"I work for you, that's all..."

"Perhaps I don't want that to be all," Hawk said silkily. Joanne's eyes were locked with his. "What about you, Joanne?" His voice was warm and deep. "What do you want?"

She wanted to tell him she wasn't interested, that he was the very last man she would get involved with, but somehow all she could do was stare at him.

"You are...tantalizing, do you know that?"

"I've always held the belief that work and play should be quite separate," Joanne said, avoiding his eyes.

"So have I. But there always has to be one exception to the rule...."

HELEN BROOKS lives in Northamptonshire, England, and is married with three children. As she is a committed Christian, busy housewife and mother, her spare time is at a premium, but her hobbies include reading and walking her two energetic and very endearing young dogs. Her long-cherished aspiration to write became a reality when she put pen to paper on reaching the age of forty, and sent the result off to Harlequin.

Books by Helen Brooks

HARLEQUIN PRESENTS®
1934—HUSBAND BY CONTRACT (Husbands & Wives #1)
1939—SECOND MARRIAGE (Husbands & Wives #2)
1987—THE MARRIAGE SOLUTION
2004—THE BABY SECRET
2021—A VERY PRIVATE REVENGE
2047—THE BRIDE'S SECRET

HELEN BROOKS

Mistletoe Mistress

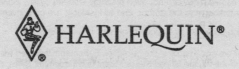

HARLEQUIN®

TORONTO • NEW YORK • LONDON
AMSTERDAM • PARIS • SYDNEY • HAMBURG
STOCKHOLM • ATHENS • TOKYO • MILAN • MADRID
PRAGUE • WARSAW • BUDAPEST • AUCKLAND

ISBN 0-373-12071-0

MISTLETOE MISTRESS

First North American Publication 1999.

Copyright © 1998 by Helen Brooks.

CHAPTER ONE

'HEY, what's with all the long faces? There hasn't been a major disaster while I've been away, has there?' Joanne's bright smile dimmed and then faded altogether as her antennae picked up the waves radiating from her office staff.

'You...you haven't heard?'

'Heard what?' Joanne's wide honey-brown eyes narrowed slightly as she repeated, 'Heard what, Maggie?'

'About what's happened.'

'*Maggie.*'

'About the takeover, and Mr Brigmore, and... everything.' Maggie wriggled slightly in her typist's chair and half turned in the seat to include the rest of the office of six, all of whom patently ignored the silent plea for help, their faces clearly stating that Maggie had started this and she could finish it.

'The takeover? Maggie, I haven't got a clue what you are talking about,' Joanne said as patiently as she could. Brusqueness never helped with Maggie; she flustered very easily. 'And where does Mr Brigmore come into all this?'

'He doesn't, not any more.' Maggie's plump plain face was very earnest, and Joanne knew she wasn't deliberately trying to be obtuse, but something of the urge she felt to wring her junior's neck must have shown on her face because Maggie added hastily, 'Mr. Brigmore's gone—early retirement or something. It all happened last Thursday, when the takeover was announced; he went the same day. I left a message on your answer machine—'

5

'I haven't been back to my flat yet; I stayed overnight with a friend…' Joanne's voice trailed away as the enormity of what Maggie was saying hit her. 'Are you telling me Mr Brigmore was axed?' she asked faintly. 'Because if you are I can't believe it. Who's stepped into his shoes, then?'

'A relation of the mogul who now owns the firm.' Maggie's voice was full of meaning and Joanne nodded silently to what remained unsaid. So, nepotism was alive and well at Concise Publications, was it? And all this had happened during the month she had been gaily backpacking round Europe on a reunion with old university friends?

She had heard about these savage 'off with the old, on with the new' mergers, where the new ruling directorate were merciless in their desire to sweep clean, but she had never actually experienced one first-hand in her eight years of working life. And Charles, of all people…

Suddenly the anger was there, hot and fierce. Charles was the fatherly figure who had given her the sort of chance, five years ago, that she had been craving since leaving university, choosing her above a host of other more qualified applicants who had been eager for the post of publishing assistant to the managing director of Concise Publications.

He had been her mentor, her champion, but most of all her friend—he and his wife, Clare, taking her under their parental wing and giving her her first real glimpse of family life. And he had been replaced? By some young upstart, no doubt, who probably didn't know one end of a book from another.

'Male or female?' Her voice was quivering, but it was with sheer fury, not weakness.

'Male.' Maggie knew how much her superior thought of their ex-managing director, and she took a deep breath before she added, 'His name is Mallen. Hawk Mallen.'

'Hawk Mallen?' Joanne's voice was scathing, her emotion blinding her to the fact that Maggie had suddenly become very still and very quiet, her eyes no longer focused on Joanne's angry face. 'What sort of name is that?'

'*My* sort of name, Ms...?'

The deep male voice was not loud, but the timbre was such that Joanne felt liquid ice run over her nerves. She didn't turn for a good thirty seconds from her position just a few inches into the room, and when she did move it was with the knowledge that she had blown it—good and proper, as Charles would have said. And she cared. Oh, not because of her job, precious and important as it had been to her up to this minute in time, she told herself bitterly, but because she had wanted to fling her resignation into the lap of this faceless bureaucrat and walk away with her head held high—not be caught out like a child telling tales out of school.

'Crawford.' Her chin was high, her golden eyes shooting sparks as she looked up into the hard dark face of the big man standing in the doorway behind her. 'And it's Miss.'

'Ah...yes, of course. Charles's elusive publishing assistant. How nice to meet you.' On face value the words were polite and courteous, but, spoken as they were, in a dark cold drawl that was both menacing and patronising, they were anything but. 'Perhaps you'd like to come through to your office so we can discuss recent events in comfort?'

He meant without the twitching ears and avid interest of the outer office, Joanne thought tightly, but for once the professionalism she prided herself on had flown out the window. 'Is there any point?' she asked stiffly, knowing she was glaring but quite unable to help herself.

The suit this man had on would have paid her salary for months, she thought bitterly, and was indicative of his sovereignty somehow. He *reeked* of wealth and power; it flowed out of every pore and was in every gesture he made. This was a man who was used to being obeyed without question. Well—tough. There was no way she was going to be intimidated by the man responsible for sacking the only person she had any real affection for in the whole wide world. Well, there was Clare too, she qualified hastily as a little stab of disloyalty to Charles's wife made itself known; she loved her too, but Charles was Charles...

'Every point, Miss Crawford.'

When, in the next moment, her elbow was taken in a firm, uncompromising grip and she found herself all but flying through the outer office and into her small but comfortable little oasis, she was too surprised to make a sound. Until the door closed behind them, that was. 'What the hell do you think you're doing?' The explosion was in line with the vibrant chestnut-red of her hair, its glowing colour a clue to the volatile temper she had battled with all her life. 'How dare you manhandle me—?'

'I'm trying to stop you making a bigger fool of yourself than you have done already,' he said with a grimness that was insulting.

'Now look—'

'*No, you look, damn it!*' It was more of a pistol shot than a bark, and as her eyes widened with shock he pushed her none too gently into the seat in front of her desk, propping himself against the dark wood and staring down at her with blazing, piercingly blue eyes. Beautiful eyes, she thought inconsequentially, before the rage took over again. 'I'm trying to do this the nice way—'

'Like you did with poor Charles?' she cut in testily, the colour in her cheeks vying with her hair.

'Give me strength...' He shut his eyes for an infinitesimal moment, raking a hand through his jet-black, very short but expertly cropped hair before saying, in a tone that was very flat and very hard, 'Do you want me to gag you? Because so help me you're a moment away from it.'

'You wouldn't dare.' But he would—she knew, without knowing how she knew, that he would.

'Try me. Just open that delectable mouth one more time before I finish saying what I want to say and try me. The pleasure, as they say, would be all mine.'

She opened her mouth to fire back an equally caustic reply, glanced at the blue silk handkerchief he had just drawn out of his breast pocket, and shut it again. The pig! The arrogant, overbearing, stinking swine—

'And I dare bet I fit most of the names that are swirling through your head right at this moment,' he drawled easily, temper and composure apparently perfectly restored, 'but unfortunately that's where they'll have to stay—in your head. Now, where were we? Oh, yes, I was trying to save you from looking ridiculous...'

She spluttered, gulped, but was forced to admit silently to herself that she didn't dare call his bluff.

He had raised dark eyebrows at her mini paroxysm but when no verbal abuse was forthcoming smiled nastily before continuing, 'Charles has left messages for you over half of Europe, there is a letter explaining the full details of the merger with Mallen Books sitting on your doorstep at home, which is repeated at length on your answer machine, but I presume, from your rather undignified outburst out there, you haven't received any of them?'

She didn't reply, and he didn't seem to expect one as he went on, 'I suggest you go home and read the letter, pop round and see Charles, do whatever it is that women do to cool down, and then we'll go from there.'

'You're dismissing me?' she asked with icy hauteur.

'Don't you ever listen?'

She had got under his skin. For all his apparent equanimity she had definitely got under his skin, she noted with some hidden satisfaction as she watched him take a deep hard pull of air before shaking his head slowly.

'You're a very intelligent woman, Miss Crawford; I know that much from your file and all that Charles has told me about you. I've seen some of your work and it's impressive, damn impressive, so what's happened during this jaunt round Europe to that noteworthy brain of yours? Are you really determined to throw your job—and the considerable salary that goes with it—to the wind on little more than a whim, a temper tantrum, because you weren't in the know when all this happened? I know Charles respects both your work and you as a person, but he had to make a fast decision on our offer and you simply weren't around to confer with. Okay?'

He thought her reaction was petulance because she hadn't been consulted about the merger? She stared at him in amazement, unable to believe she was hearing right.

'Okay?' he said again, his voice cool and biting.

'Mr Mallen, I couldn't care less if you took over this firm and a hundred others besides every day for a month,' she said furiously. 'That's not the issue here.'

'Really?' He smiled a smile that wasn't a smile at all.

'Yes, really.' She had never wanted to wipe a smile from someone's face so violently before. 'The only thing that concerns me is the way you've got rid of Charles. This firm was his lifeblood, his reason for living, and don't tell me I don't know what I'm talking about,' she warned testily as he opened his mouth to interrupt. 'I know Charles—I know him better than you for a start—and to leave this firm would be like leaving his own child. He built Concise Publications up from nothing, sacrificed for it, lived his life around it, and now you sweep in and throw him out as though he's nothing.'

'You've got this all wrong—'

'Oh, spare me.' He wasn't used to being spoken to like this, and his displeasure was evident in the narrowing of the brilliant blue eyes and hard line of his mouth. A sensual mouth, firm and full, with a sexy bottom lip— She caught the thought as it materialised, shocked to the core at its inappropriateness, and it made her voice harsh as she went on, 'You've got rid of Charles and I don't doubt for a minute that he won't be the last to go. Well, I'll make it easy for you, Mr Mallen, and resign right now. I've no wish to continue working under the new administration, okay?'

The last word was said with exactly the same emphasis he had placed on it a few moments earlier and spoke of her utter disgust more strongly than anything she had said before.

'I don't believe I'm having this conversation.' As Joanne went to rise he pushed her back down in the seat with a mite more force than was necessary. 'And sit still, damn it,' he growled angrily. 'I haven't finished yet.'

'But I have.' This time when she rose he let her, his eyes unblinking as she smoothed down the pencil-slim skirt over her hips and tugged the matching jacket into place with shaking hands. He was a brute of a man, a cold, arrogant tyrant. She'd seen plenty of the same since coming to London from her university in Manchester eight years ago, and had never stopped thanking the guardian angel who had led her to Concise Publications and the Brigmores. She couldn't have wished for a better boss, and Clare had become more than a friend, almost a mother...

'How can someone who looks so fragile be so impossible?' he asked with a quietness that had all the softness of tempered steel. 'I've met some troublesome females in my time but you take the biscuit hands down.' He had straightened as she'd stood, and now she became

fully aware for the first time of his considerable height
and bulk, his broad-shouldered, lean body towering over
her five feet six inches in a way that made her feel positively minute. And she was aware of something else too,
something…undefinable, magnetic that pulsed from the
hard male frame with a drawing power that was formidable, and it was this that made her swing round on her
heel and make for the door without another word.

'Is that it?'

In any other circumstance, with any other man, the
look of utter surprise on his face as she turned round
would have made her smile; as it was she stared at him
for a moment before she said, 'There's no point in continuing this, is there?'

'You really intend to throw in the towel because you
consider Charles has been hard done by?' He surveyed
her cynically, his mouth hard. 'What sort of relationship
did you have with your departed boss anyway?' he
added silkily, his meaning plain.

'I don't even intend to acknowledge that with the fa-
vour of a reply,' she said icily, her eyes wishing him
somewhere very hot and very final as she glared at him
one more time, before opening the door and sweeping
into the outer office with a regality that wasn't lost on
Hawk Mallen as he watched her go.

He liked her style. He watched her cross the outer
office and exit without turning her head or faltering in
her purpose. Yes, whatever else, she had one hell of a
way with her.

Once in the corridor outside, Joanne set her face in a
practised smile and made for the lift, passing the other
offices on the exalted top floor of Concise Publications
without looking to left or right. There were three floors
in all, and as the lift took her swiftly downwards Joanne
found she had gone into automatic, her whole being concentrating on getting out of the building and into her car

without the humiliation of breaking down. One of Charles's editors—no, not Charles's any more, she corrected herself painfully—was in Reception and raised a hand to her as she passed. 'Everything all right?'

'Fine, fine.' She smiled and nodded but didn't stop, her mind registering the stupidity of her reply in the circumstances.

Once in her snazzy little red car she sat for a whole minute just breathing deeply before she could persuade her shaking hands to start the engine. Her whole life, the interesting, vital life she had fought for so hard, had just been turned upside down and the shock waves had her head buzzing.

She should have phoned Clare and Charles last night—she had meant to—but her flight from France had been delayed and when Melanie had offered her a bed for the night, rather than her having to drive right across London in the rush hour to her flat, she'd accepted gratefully. And then she had had a bath, and they'd eaten, and consumed one of the bottles of wine they'd brought back between them...

'Damn, damn, damn...' She turned and glanced at her huge rucksack in the middle of the back seat, surrounded by bags of wine and boxes of Belgian chocolates she'd brought back as presents, and then slipped off the jacket to the suit she had borrowed from Melanie and flung it on the seat beside her as she started the engine. Well, it was too late now; she had quite literally walked into the lion's mouth and definitely come off the worse for wear, but the main thing was to touch base with Charles and see how he was. It was so ironic that all this had happened during the first real holiday she had had in years, she thought miserably as she steered the car out of her reserved space in Concise Publication's small car park, and on to the busy main road.

The urge to see Charles was overwhelming, and as his

house in Islington was on her route home she headed for there, forcing herself to concentrate on the morning traffic rather than her jumbled thoughts that were flying in all directions. The September day was balmy and mellow, the warm sunshine pleasant but lacking the fierce heat that had characterised July and August, but Joanne was oblivious to the weather as she drove through the London streets in a turmoil that made her soft full mouth tight and stained her creamy, sun-tinted skin an angry red.

It was ten o'clock when she drew up outside Charles and Clare's large three-storeyed terraced house in its wide and pleasant street, and by five past she was seated in a cushioned cane chair in the garden with a box of tissues at her elbow and a steaming cup of coffee in front of her. 'I'm sorry, I didn't mean to cry on you...'

Clare, who was sitting on the arm of Joanne's chair, pulled her closer to her maternal bosom as Charles tut-tutted from his vantage point opposite. 'It's our fault, Joanne; it must have been such a shock to you,' Clare said worriedly. 'But apart from leaving a message for you to ring us when you got home, and the letter, of course, we didn't know how to contact you. The postcards kept coming from somewhere different every few days. Did you have a nice time?' she added as an after-thought.

'Lovely.' Joanne dismissed the month of fun and laughter in one word.

'And you only found out about the merger when you went in this morning?' Clare enquired anxiously.

Joanne nodded. She had only been able to blurt that much out on the doorstep before bursting into tears, from which point it had been all action.

'And did Hawk Mallen explain it fully?' Charles asked now. 'I couldn't have refused, Jo; offers like that don't come every day. Besides which...' He paused, glancing at Clare who nodded encouragingly. 'I haven't been too well recently and this seemed to present itself as a chance to get out of the rat race and have a few years enjoying ourselves before we're too old.'

'What do you mean, not too well?' Joanne knew Charles; he would rather walk through coals of fire than ever admit he was less than one hundred per cent fit. It was something she and Clare, along with the couple's three children, called his obstinate streak.

'We haven't told the children, for the same reason we didn't tell you—you'd all worry yourselves to death. But that time three months ago when Charles had a week off with flu—it was a minor heart attack. Very minor,' Clare added hastily as Joanne's eyes shot to Charles's sheepish face, 'but I've persuaded him to take it as a warning, and when this offer from the Mallen Corporation came along it seemed like the answer to everything.'

'Why didn't you tell me about the heart attack?' Joanne asked faintly. 'I could have helped.'

'*I* wanted to,' Clare said quickly, 'but you know Charles. He loves you like one of our own, Joanne, and he didn't want any of you worried—'

'Or fussing,' Charles cut in wryly. 'Clare did all the fussing that was necessary, believe me.'

'How long has this takeover been in the offing?' Joanne asked numbly, feeling as though the ground was moving under her feet. Charles was ill, with heart trouble? *Charles?*

'There has been the odd feeler there for a couple of months,' Charles said quietly, 'but the thing only crystallised the week you left for Europe. The Mallen Corporation is huge—I don't know if Hawk explained to you, but the publishing side is just one of their interests. When the offer became concrete I jumped at it, it's as simple as that really, and I decided to cut the umbilical cord in the process.

'Hawk Mallen is old man Mallen's grandson and right-hand man; apart from knowing everything there is to know about publishing, he's a brilliant businessman and entrepreneur—something I've never pretended to be,' he added drily. 'He's the future, I'm the past; if I had stayed I would have got in his way and that wouldn't have been good for either of us. He's a ruthless so-and-so, but he's got what it takes, Jo; you can't fault the man on business acumen.'

'I see.' As Charles went on, explaining the details of the transaction and the part everyone had played in it, Joanne's heart sank deeper and deeper.

It had been Charles who had insisted on the opt-out clause, Charles who had wanted to walk away at once without any long-drawn-out and heart-rending, mentally exhausting valedictions. And she'd accused Hawk Mallen of... She inwardly squirmed as she remembered the exact charges she'd laid at his feet. Oh, what a mess, what a terrible, almost laughable mess. Thank goodness she could rely on Charles for a good reference because she sure as eggs wouldn't get one from the eminent Mr Mallen.

If he wasn't as mad as hell at her, he'd be laughing his head off, and of the two options she'd much prefer the former, she thought painfully as a pair of piercingly blue cold eyes set in a hard, uncompromising face swam into the screen of her mind. But fortunately she'd never know one way or the other anyway, having burnt her bridges so completely.

And now she would have to tell Clare and Charles...

They were upset, horrified, bewildered—blaming themselves, Hawk Mallen, anyone but Joanne—but by the time she left their tranquil home, after an alfresco lunch under the clear September sky, she had their solemn promise not to try to get her reinstated in any way.

She had made her bed and she would lie on it, she

thought determinedly on the drive home, and maybe it was time for a change anyway. She was twenty-nine years of age, and after the years of exams and striving for her degree she had only had two jobs—one of which was Concise Publications—and had hardly seen anything of life. The trip round Europe these past weeks had opened her eyes to the fact that there was a big wide world out there, just waiting to be explored, and perhaps this was the nudge she needed to get moving?

She had been happy and safe the last few years, Charles and Clare's open-armed drawing of her into their family going some way to heal the hurts of the past, but whilst she was cocooned in such a protected environment she would never reach out for more. And she wanted more.

The thought was a surprise, opening her eyes wide for an instant as she considered it. But it was true. Not the bonds of matrimony or a husband—she felt the panic and fear that accompanied such a possibility wash over her before she thrust them back behind the closed door in her mind—but she wanted to travel, to see new places, new cultures, work in different environments. And she could do it; *she could*. As Charles had said, the umbilical cord had been cut, nothing would be the same again, so *now* was the time.

Her spacious one-bedroom flat on the top storey of an old renovated house overlooking myriad rooftops and a wide expanse of light washed sky welcomed her as she opened the front door, the large terracotta-tiled balcony where she ate most of her meals during the spring and summer causing a momentary hiccup in her plans. Could she leave it? This, her first real home where she had been so happy, so secure?

She opened the French windows from the high-ceilinged lounge and walked out on to the flower-bedecked balcony, noting that most of the plants festooning the walls and floor were alive and thriving, for which she had to thank her neighbour on the floor below who had promised faithfully to water them each evening.

She was brought from further musing by the strident ringing of the telephone in the room she had just left and hurried back indoors, lifting the receiver and speaking breathlessly as she gave the number, fully expecting it to be Clare making sure she had reached home safely after the emotion of the day.

It wasn't Clare.

'Miss Crawford?' The deep dark voice was unmistakable. 'This is Hawk Mallen.'

'I... What...? Yes, Mr Mallen?' Oh, pull yourself together, for goodness' sake, she thought scathingly as she heard her faltering voice with a burst of self-contempt that was humiliating. What *did* she sound like? But she sat down very suddenly on the little pouffe next to the phone, her legs turning to jelly.

'Are you in full possession of all the facts relating to the takeover of Concise Publications by Mallen Books now?' the male voice, with its almost gravelly texture, asked expressionlessly.

'I think... I think so, and I just want to say I didn't realise... That is, I know I spoke out of turn—'

'Miss Crawford, I didn't ring for an apology, if that's what you are thinking, although it is acknowledged and accepted.'

She blinked a little, even more glad she was sitting down as her stomach turned over with a shuddering jerk. He was terrifying—in spite of the miles separating them that dark, formidable aura swept into the room along with his voice and caused her nerves to go haywire.

Once Charles had accepted she was serious about not going back he had related numerous stories about the Mallen empire, most of them featuring Hawk Mallen, and as she had listened she had known that even if today had not happened she could not have worked for this single-minded, utterly frightening, ruthless tycoon. He was the original workaholic according to Charles—cold, untouchable, his reputation built purely by his own efforts and having nothing to do with his grandfather's name. As Charles had gone on the main element to her emotion was sheer wonder that she had dared to say all she had to this walking legend. No wonder he had looked so amazed as she had left; it was doubtful if anyone had ever spoken to him like that before, or walked out on him either.

'Miss Crawford? Are you still there?'

She realised she was sitting in a kind of trance and jerked to life with the voice in her ear. 'Yes, yes, I am.' Breathe deeply, talk coherently, *act your age*. 'Thank you—'

'I would like to see you privately; I think the office staff have been entertained enough for one day,' he said silkily, his voice so smooth and bland that for a moment the import of his words didn't strike home. 'And preferably before the day starts tomorrow. Would this evening be convenient?'

'This evening?' Her voice was a squeak of horror—she knew it and he must have heard it, and now she began to gabble in an effort to cover up. 'I don't think so. I've just got back from holiday, you see, and there are things to do. I really can't—'

'Shall we say eight o'clock?' The silkiness sheathed cold steel, but in spite of his intimidation a little spurt of anger at his arrogance rose, hot and fierce.

'I honestly don't think there is any point, Mr Mallen.' Her voice was firmer but she was still glad she was sitting down. 'I can call by the office at your convenience to pick up my salary cheque and clear any outstanding matters you might need my assistance on; I'm quite prepared to help—'

'In that case you will see me this evening,' he said coolly. 'I'm not asking you for a date—' there was a moment's pause when she felt herself flush bright scarlet '—merely suggesting we discuss certain business matters over dinner.'

'But—'

'That's settled, then. Eight it is.' And the phone went dead. She stared at it for a full minute—the deep voice with its faint American accent still ringing in her ears—before she slowly replaced the receiver, but even then she made no effort to stand. He was taking her out to dinner? Hawk Mallen? Taking *her* out to dinner? She couldn't; she just couldn't.

She picked up the phone again and dialled Charles's number, her hand shaking.

'Charles Brigmore?' His voice was so reassuringly familiar she wanted to cry again, but checked the impulse firmly. She couldn't remember the last time she had cried before today, and now she couldn't stop.

'Charles, you'll never guess what's happened...' There was complete silence at the other end of the line as she went on, and as the silence lengthened when she had finished she said hesitantly, 'Charles? Say something.'

'You've agreed to go out to dinner with Hawk Mallen?' Charles asked bemusedly. 'But...why?'

'I didn't exactly *agree* to anything,' Joanne said a trifle testily. 'I told you. He just sort of...told me.'

'Well, untell him,' Charles said with a surprising lack of grammar. 'You don't know what you are getting into, Jo.'

'I *do*.' She paused, and moderated her tone as she continued, 'I've an idea anyway; that's why I'm ringing you to discuss it. I don't know why he wants to see me, but after my little outburst today it can't be for anything good. He wasn't too pleased when I left.'

'I can imagine.' Charles's voice was very dry.

'He can't hold me to anything, can he, with my contract?' Joanne asked anxiously. 'I know it says three months' notice, but surely in the circumstances he'd be prepared to be reasonable?'

'I don't think "reasonable" is a word that features in Hawk Mallen's vocabulary,' Charles said slowly. 'Look, ring him back and ask him exactly what he wants to see you about. That's only sensible, and if you're still not happy...'

'I shan't be happy; of course I shan't be happy,' Joanne said flatly. 'Would you be happy going out to dinner with Hawk Mallen after speaking to him the way I did? He's probably after my blood.'

'As long as that's all he's after,' Charles said darkly.

'What do you mean?'

'Joanne...' Charles's voice held the patience that characterised his relationship with her. 'I know you don't preen and powder like the average female but you must look in the mirror sometimes, surely? You're a very attractive woman, and Hawk Mallen is definitely very much a man. I didn't say this this afternoon, but he doesn't only work hard, if you get my meaning; the play is done pretty energetically and with great effect too.'

'No, he made it clear it wasn't a date, Charles; he actually spelled it out. Besides which I hardly think someone like Hawk Mallen would look twice at me.' She smiled to herself at the thought. 'He must have his pick of women.'

'No doubt,' Charles said drily.

'But I will phone him back. I can't see any point in meeting him,' she said resolutely.

'Ring me if there's any trouble.'

There was trouble, but she didn't ring back, deciding that it was her problem, not Charles's. Hawk Mallen wasn't in the building, Sue on Reception told her politely, and no, she had no idea where he could be contacted. She could give her the name of the hotel where he was staying at present if she'd like to ring there? Joanne did like, but he wasn't there either. She left messages in both places for him to contact her if he returned, and then paced the floor for the rest of the afternoon waiting for the telephone to ring.

By six o'clock she was panicking badly; by seven she had had a bath and washed her hair, and a feeling of inevitability had settled over her like a blanket. Whether he'd got her messages or not he wouldn't ring; she should have known, she told herself resignedly. He had made up his mind he was going to talk to her tonight, and that, as far as he was concerned, was that.

What did one wear when going out to dinner with a megalomaniac? she asked herself helplessly as she surveyed her wardrobe. Especially a fabulously wealthy, dark, attractive one, who frightened her half to death and was probably gunning for her blood? Was he going to prove awkward? Take pleasure in telling her he was going to put the knife in with future employers and so on? Or was he going to hold her to every last day of her contract? She could leave anyway—it would just mean a loss of salary and other benefits—but it wouldn't look too good with prospective employers.

The carefree days of the last month seemed like another lifetime as she glumly pulled a high-necked, long-sleeved cocktail dress in crushed black silk off its hanger. The dress was expensive but the style demure; it gave the impression of a controlled, capable woman in charge of her own destiny, which was exactly what she wanted for the night ahead.

Her hair was trimmed in a sleek bob just above the nape and she normally wore it loose, but she needed the extra sophistication having it up would give her, she decided nervously as she glanced at her reflection in the mirror. She was all fingers and thumbs, but eventually it was secured in a neat chignon at the back of her head, a pair of tiny gold studs her only jewellery, and a touch of mascara the sum total of her make-up.

There—calm, cool and competent, she decided silently as she looked into the long full-length mirror in her bedroom, seeing only the elegant dress with its matching shoes, and quite missing the beauty of her glowing red hair and honey-brown eyes which complemented the black silk perfectly.

Hawk Mallen missed neither when Joanne opened the door to his knock at exactly eight o'clock, her colour high again as she saw him framed in the doorway, big and dark and lazily self-assured.

'I've been trying to contact you all afternoon.' It probably wasn't the best of opening lines, but her brain seemed to scramble at the sight or sound of this man.

'And now you have.' He smiled easily, but it didn't reach the riveting blue eyes and she knew instantly, without a shadow of a doubt, that he had received her messages and guessed the reason for them.

'I...I was just going to ask what this was all about.' She had raised her chin slightly as she spoke without being aware of it, and the subtle gesture spoke volumes to the man watching her so closely.

'All in good time.' He gestured to the room beyond. 'Do you have a wrap, a jacket...?'

'Yes. Oh, come in.' She stepped back so hastily she nearly pivoted on the three-inch heels which were much higher than those she normally wore, recovering herself just in time and feeling her face grow even hotter in the process. This was going to be a riot of an evening, she told herself desperately, walking carefully through the tiny square hall and into the lounge where she had placed her jacket and handbag. She couldn't even stay upright, let alone impress him with her woman-of-the-world persona.

'Nice flat.' He had followed her, and as she turned the room immediately shrank in deference to his presence, his impressive height and build seeming to fill the pleasant light surroundings.

'I like it.' She couldn't for the life of her manage her normal social smile as she stared at him before moving hastily away, her face still flaming, and busying herself adjusting the brilliance of the wall lights. She reached for her jacket and bag. 'Shall we?' She nodded to the front door but he didn't move, surveying her with cool, narrowed eyes for a long, heart-thudding moment.

'I'm not going to eat you, you know,' he said softly. 'You're not Little Red Riding Hood and I'm not the Wolf. Well...' He paused, his eyes narrowing still more. 'You're not Little Red Riding Hood anyway,' he added sardonically.

'I didn't say—'

'You didn't have to.' He interrupted her before she could finish and again the incredible self-assurance hit a nerve.

'Mr Mallen—'

'Hawk, please,' he interjected softly.

'Mr Mallen, I've no idea what was so important that it couldn't wait until normal office hours, but I really don't think this is a good idea,' she said stiffly. 'I tried to contact you this afternoon—'

'You've already said that.' The dark eyebrows rose mockingly.

'But you clearly didn't receive my messages,' she finished a trifle desperately. This was awful; *he* was awful.

'Oh, I did, both of them, but I chose to ignore them,' he said easily, his voice as pleasant as if he were discussing the weather.

'You what?' She couldn't match his calm, her voice high.

'Ignored them.' He smiled maliciously, clearly thoroughly enjoying her open-mouthed discomfiture. 'You suspected that, didn't you?' he added silkily. 'But you expected me to lie to you. I never lie, Joanne. When you know me better you will appreciate that is the truth. However painful, however costly, I never lie.'

Know him better? Over her dead body!

'Now, there is a table booked at the Maltese Inn for nine, so if you're ready?'

The dark face was expressionless, the blue eyes unwavering, and as she gazed into the hard, implacable features she conceded defeat. Okay, she'd go on this wretched evening out, she could hardly do anything else now, but there was no way she was going to be bullied or threatened by this man, whatever his wealth or connections.

'Yes, I'm quite ready.' She looked at him steadily, trying to hide the fact that she felt like a petrified little rabbit in the hypnotising power of a fox, and even managed a tight smile as she said, 'I'm just worried that this evening will be a lamentable waste of your valuable time, Mr Mallen.'

'Why don't you let me worry about that?' he said quietly. 'And I told you, the name's Hawk.'

Hawk. Yes, the name suited him, she thought with a faint touch of hysteria as he took her arm and ushered her out of the flat. She had been mistaken in her analogy of a fox; he was far more like the ruthless, keen-sighted bird of prey he had been named after, and at the moment she had the awful conviction that the quarry in his sights was her!

CHAPTER TWO

THE Maltese Inn was an exclusive little nightclub she had heard about but never had the necessary connections to enter, it being the haunt of the very rich and the very famous. It was chic, select, and its clientele ranged from wealthy film stars and top models to the very élite of England's aristocracy.

Once in Hawk's car, which just had to be a magnificent sporty monster she had never heard of before but which was undoubtedly in the super league—nothing as well known as a Ferrari or Lamborghini for him, she thought nastily—she found herself dumb with nerves.

She glanced at him several times from under her eyelashes, her eyes and senses registering the big lean body clothed in evening dress with a jolt that didn't lessen with the third or fourth glance, before forcing herself to make some sort of conversation. 'This is a beautiful car.' Never had words been so inadequate; never had she *felt* so inadequate. 'What is it?'

'A Cizeta-Moroder V16T.' The piercing eyes flashed over her face for a moment before returning to the windscreen.

'Oh.' She was no nearer and it showed.

'It's an Italian car, designed by Marcello Gandini,' Hawk said easily. 'I like the power, the body style, and it's beautiful and fast. When I drive I like to enjoy the experience, besides which I wanted a car which would take me from A to B in as short a time as possible.'

'And this certainly would.' She glanced round the interior of the two-seater coupé which was as dynamic inside as out.

'I also like unusual things, not necessarily unique but things that haven't been...cheapened by overuse,' he continued softly.

There had been a thread of something in his voice she couldn't quite place, but as she glanced at the dark profile again it gave nothing away, his features relaxed and quite expressionless.

She couldn't believe she was sitting in the sort of car one only saw in the movies, being driven to the most fashionable nightclub in London by a dark, handsome— No, not handsome. She caught her thoughts abruptly, sneaking another glance at him. Handsome was too weak a word somehow for Hawk Mallen; it suggested pretty-boy good looks, traditional appeal, and the lean, hard face, penetrating blue eyes and cruel, sensual mouth were anything but that. She shivered suddenly, in spite of the perfectly regulated temperature within the car.

What on earth was she doing here? She must be mad. Her thoughts did nothing to calm her racing heartbeat. And the Maltese Inn, of all places. It was all Diors and diamonds there, and here was she in her little black dress and off-the-peg jacket... She felt a moment of nausea as her stomach turned right over. She was going to stand out like a sore thumb—

'Look, could you just try and think of me as friend and not foe for an hour or two, at least until the meal is over?' The deep, gravelly voice had amusement at its core; she could hear it curling the edges. 'Good food is life's second greatest pleasure...' The piercing gaze swept over her flushed face for one brief moment but it left her in no doubt as to what he considered the first, and she felt herself blush even more fiercely. 'And I'd prefer to enjoy the meal tonight without indigestion at the end of it.'

'I don't know you, Mr Mallen—Hawk,' she corrected

hastily as he made a growl of annoyance in his throat, 'so how could I possibly regard you as foe?'

'I've been involved with a good few women in my time, Joanne, on a business level and otherwise,' he said quietly, 'and one thing I've learnt along the way is that your sex doesn't need a reason for anything it feels like doing.'

'Well, that's a sexist remark if ever I heard one,' she retorted scathingly, forgetting her nervousness and apprehension as he pressed the fire button. 'You're one of those men who think women are empty-headed little dolls, good for one thing only?'

'Did I say that?' he drawled softly.

'You didn't have to.' She was trying to give the impression of being as controlled and calm as he was, but it was difficult—more than difficult. She might have known he'd be a male chauvinist pig on top of everything else; this was getting worse by the minute.

'You might have been able to read Charles's mind but not mine, Joanne,' he said calmly, 'so please don't make the mistake of thinking you can. And I wasn't insinuating anything about Charles, before further crimes are laid at my feet. I'm quite aware of the platonic relationship between you both—''a father and daughter affection'' were the words used to explain it, I think,' he said easily, 'by none other than his wife.'

'You asked *Clare* about me?' she screeched, her voice reverberating around the car's plush interior and causing the man at the wheel to wince visibly. 'How dare you?'

'Who better to ask?' His sidelong glance took in her scarlet face and he actually chuckled before adding, 'Calm down, Joanne, calm down; it wasn't like that. On the way to pick you up this evening I called by Charles's house with some papers for him to sign, and it was Clare who mentioned you as it happens. They're very fond of you, aren't they?' he said quietly. 'You're quite one of the family.'

She wasn't sure if he was being nasty or not but her temper was still at boiling point and she didn't trust herself to speak anyway. What an impossible man, she thought angrily. If ever she had needed confirmation that her decision to leave Concise Publications had been the right one, she'd just had it. Working as Charles's publishing assistant had been nothing but pleasure, but as Hawk Mallen's...

'Did you enjoy your job, Joanne?' It was as though he had read her mind, and she noted the past tense with a little flutter in her stomach. So, she *was* out on her car, but then why this dinner tonight? she thought bitterly. So he could gloat, was that it?

'Yes, I did.' In spite of all her efforts to the contrary she couldn't quite keep the thread of antagonism from showing. 'It was interesting, exciting.'

'And from what Charles tells me your input was considerably more than one could normally expect from a publishing assistant; would you say that was fair?' he asked mildly.

She shrugged carefully. 'I've no personal commitments so there was no need to clock-watch if that's what you mean.'

'Not exactly.' The sleek, low beast of a car had just growled reluctantly to a halt at some traffic lights, and he stretched in the leather seat as he waited for amber, the movement bringing powerfully muscled thighs disconcertingly into her consciousness as she glanced his way. Her head shot to the front as though she had been bitten, the colour that had just begun to recede surging into her cheeks again.

What *was* it about him? she asked herself helplessly. Sexual magnetism? The aphrodisiac of wealth and power and authority? Sheer old-fashioned sex appeal? It was all those things and more, and it was devastating. He would have been dynamite on the silver screen, she thought ruefully. Pure twenty-four-carat box-office dynamite.

He didn't speak again as the Cizeta-Moroder sprang away from the lights, but as they travelled along the well-lit London streets her nerve-endings were screaming at her awareness of him, and she had never felt so out of her depth in all her life.

When they drew up outside the refined elegant building of the Maltese Inn he uncoiled his big body from the low-slung car with easy animal grace, moving to the passenger side in a moment and opening her door for her.

'You aren't going to leave it here?' She stared at him in surprise once she was on the pavement, but in the next second a massive uniformed doorman, who looked more like a prize fighter than anything else, was at their side.

'Keys, Bob.' Hawk dropped the keys into the man's outstretched hand with a warm smile along with a folded banknote. 'Look after her.'

'As always, Mr Mallen, as always. Good evening, miss.'

'Good evening.' Joanne smiled into the big ugly face with a naturalness that had been missing in her dealings with Hawk, something the piercing blue eyes noted and filed.

There was another doorman ready to open the gleaming plate-glass door into the entrance lobby, and another who ushered them through that and into the area beyond, where the reception area, powder rooms and cloakrooms were, the nightclub itself being up a flight of wide, graciously curved stairs that would have done credit to any Hollywood movie.

Having divested herself of her jacket, Joanne was

painfully conscious of the plainness of her dress and jewellery as she joined Hawk, the surrounding area seeming full of glittering women, with diamonds on their wrists, throat and ears, and all wearing dresses that must have cost a small fortune.

She was aware of the subdued buzz that Hawk was drawing, especially from the female contingent, as they walked towards the stairs, and it took all her will-power to keep her head high and her face cool and contained as they climbed the marble steps to the nightclub beyond.

That Hawk himself had noticed the covert glances became apparent when, on reaching the top of the stairs, he leant down and whispered in her ear, 'Don't worry, they are the same with everyone; they're trying to work out what us being together means.'

They aren't the only ones, Joanne thought wryly, her nerves as tight as piano wire.

'Too much time and too much money breeds mischief,' Hawk went on cynically, 'as many a damaged reputation has discovered.'

'I wouldn't know.' She glanced back down into the glittering array beneath them as they turned to go through the doors into the dimly lit nightclub, and there was more than one pair of beautifully painted eyes that stared brazenly back at her.

'You don't gossip?'

It was said mockingly but with more than a touch of scepticism, and Joanne paused just inside the room, meeting his sardonic gaze as she said, 'No, I don't. Why? Is that so unbelievable?'

'Yes.' The sensual mouth quirked apologetically. 'I told you I don't lie,' he continued softly, 'and you did ask.'

'You seem to have a very low opinion of the female sex, Mr Mallen,' she said tightly. 'Or am I mistaken?'

It was a direct confrontation, and he smiled slowly, his eyes turning to liquid silver under the muted lighting and his dark skin accentuated by the whiteness of his smile. 'I can't answer that on the grounds that it might incriminate me,' he said lightly.

'I see.' She was about to say more, a lot more, but the appearance of the head waiter, with a smile as wide as London Bridge, put paid to the flood of angry words, and as they were led to what was obviously a superior table, right on the edge of the large dance-floor, she found herself once again overawed by her surroundings.

The champagne cocktails that appeared as though by magic at their elbows the moment they were seated were absolutely delicious; in fact she hadn't tasted anything quite so delicious before, but she noticed that although Hawk ordered a second for her he had nothing more exciting than mineral water.

'I'm driving.' He answered her raised eyebrows with a smile. 'One is enough.'

'How resolute of you,' she answered lightly.

'Not really.' The blue eyes narrowed, his gaze intent as he said, 'My father had three times the permitted level of alcohol in his blood when he went off the road and caused the death of himself and my mother fifteen years ago. He was forty-four, she was just forty; I don't find it hard to say no to alcohol when I'm driving.'

'I'm sorry.' She didn't know what else to say. 'Have you any brothers or sisters?' she asked lamely.

'No.' He didn't elaborate. 'How about you? Do you come from a big family?' he asked quietly.

'No.' She hadn't expected this and it took her completely by surprise, causing her to stammer slightly as she said, 'My...my mother is dead and I never knew my father.'

'No siblings?' The keen eyes had narrowed on her flushed face.

'No, I...I was brought up in foster homes mostly. My mother...she didn't relate too well to children.' She stopped abruptly, appalled at what she had revealed. This man had drawn out of her what it had taken Charles and Clare twelve months to achieve. How could she have told him that about her childhood? she asked herself desperately. It had sounded as though she was asking for sympathy and that was the last thing, the very last thing, she wanted.

The appearance of a waiter at Hawk's elbow in the next moment eased the situation somewhat, and after they had ordered he didn't comment about what had been said before, engaging her in light, easy conversation that taxed neither her brain nor her tongue.

But... And there was a but, she thought silently, even as she laughed at something witty, and faintly cruel, he had just said about a well-known television presenter who had just swept into the nightclub with all the regality of royalty. Yes, there definitely was a but, although she couldn't quite determine what it was.

Possibly the way he was watching her, his blue eyes cynical and probing even as his mouth smiled and made small talk, or perhaps it was the rather remote way he had with him, as though he was surveying everything and everyone from a distance and finding them wanting. Whatever, it was disconcerting, unnerving, and she was immensely glad of the fortifying cocktails to quieten the rampant butterflies in her stomach that had been fluttering crazily since she had first opened the door of the flat to him.

The meal was delicious, but she found each mouthful an effort, mainly because as people finished eating and began to take to the dance-floor she realised the moment Hawk would ask her to dance was imminent.

He seemed in no hurry to explain why he had asked to see her; every time she had tried to broach the matter he had changed the subject with a firmness that was daunting, and now dessert was nearly finished and, short of asking for a second helping, which would only delay the inevitable, there was no escape. And she didn't want to dance with him; in fact the thought of him touching her, however circumspectly, was...disturbing. She finished the last mouthful of chocolate soufflé—it had been hovering in its dish for minutes and she really couldn't delay any longer—and almost in the same instant he stood, bending over her and drawing her to her feet before she could protest.

'You can't come to the Inn and not dance; it really isn't done,' he said in a deep mocking whisper that told her he had been fully aware of her thoughts and had taken what he considered to be the appropriate action.

'Perhaps I don't care about what's done,' she muttered quietly as she found herself on the dance-floor, stiffening helplessly as his arms enclosed her.

'Perhaps you don't.' The frighteningly perceptive eyes ran over her flushed face before he said, his voice low but alive with wicked amusement, 'Or perhaps it's me? It's all right, Joanne, my ego can survive—just—if you confirm my worst fears.'

'Which are?' she asked tightly, her body desperately aware of the hard male frame close to hers and the undeniably delicious masculine fragrance emanating from the tanned skin.

'That you don't like me?'

'Am I supposed to like you?' she asked shakily.

'Of course.' The arrogance was full of self-mockery which increased her turmoil. He wasn't supposed to laugh at himself; that didn't fit the image. 'Every woman I meet is automatically bowled over by my charm and pleasing countenance, not to mention my wealth,' he added darkly.

'You think they are just after your money?' she asked

in amazement. Even the most hardened gold-digger would rock on her heels when confronted by the male-ness of Hawk Mallen.

'I think it oils the wheels.' He smiled, but it was a mere twisting of the cruel, sensual mouth and not really a smile at all.

'That's…that's—'

'Realistic.' He cut into her shocked stammering with a lazy drawl, pulling her a little closer as he did so.

'*Awful.*' She stared up at him, her cheeks hot. 'You can't lump the whole female race into one package like that.'

'Can't I?' He considered her for a long quiet moment before smiling again. 'Why not?' he asked softly.

'Because everyone's different; people have different values, different perspectives— Oh, you *know* why not,' she finished tightly, not at all sure if he was teasing her or if he meant what he had said.

'Your personnel file says you are twenty-nine years old, right?' He looked down at her, his dark face un-readable.

She nodded, wondering what was coming next.

'And you have never married.' It was a flat statement. 'Lived with anyone?' he asked quietly.

'That's nothing to do with you.' She struggled slightly in his hold, resenting the personal questioning, but all he did was pull her even closer, settling her against the broad expanse of his chest, his chin nuzzling the red silk of her hair.

'Have you lived with anyone, Joanne?' he asked again, his voice still soft but threaded through with a silky coolness that told her he was determined to have an answer.

'No.' It was useless to fight him but she bitterly re-sented the interrogation.

'And according to Charles you don't date much—rarely in fact,' he said thoughtfully. 'Very rarely.'

'Did Charles say that?' She was deeply offended and hurt at Charles's betrayal.

'No.' She would have jerked away again but the arms holding her were forged in steel. 'But I'm very adept at reading between the lines and I know the sort of questions to ask that give me the answers I require,' he said easily.

'How clever of you,' she snapped nastily.

'Isn't it?' He moved her slightly from him now, keeping her within the circle of his arms as he looked down at her with hard, narrowed eyes. 'Now I'd say, on a likelihood of ten to one, that you have—how did you put it? Oh, yes—"lumped" the whole male race together fairly successfully.' His tone had lost any amusement, his face absolutely straight as he added, 'Or am I wrong?'

'Quite wrong,' she said cuttingly, her face flaming.

'Oh, Joanne. Joanne, Joanne...' He shook his head sorrowfully, the mockery back. 'And here's me being honest and above board—'

'Are you insinuating I'm not?' she asked hotly.

'Absolutely.' And then he grinned, and all further opposition left her in a big whoosh as she absorbed the difference to his face that his first real smile made. He was devastating, gorgeous, overwhelming... She swallowed hard and prayed for the ground to stop rippling under her feet. He was a man, just a man, and an arrogant, self-satisfied pig of one at that. He'd just lost her her job, hadn't he? She *couldn't* be attracted to him; what was the matter with her, for goodness' sake—?

'But I forgive you.' He had pulled her close again and, mainly because her legs suddenly seemed to have the consistency of melted jelly, she didn't resist.

However, she managed a fairly tart, 'How very gracious of you,' which brought an answering chuckle from above her head, before they continued to dance in silence. It was a slow number—of course it had to be, she thought caustically; even the band was against her—and although she desperately wanted to seem immune to what his body was doing to hers she could feel herself begin to tremble in his arms.

'What's happened in your life to make you so afraid of physical contact?' he murmured after several humiliating minutes when she knew her shaking had made itself obvious. 'I'm not going to hurt you, Joanne. Trust me.'

'Trust you?' She was inexpressibly thankful that he had misread her body's reaction to his, although there was more than a little fear mixed up in the mortifying sexual excitement that had her in its grip. And now, as the music changed, and she saw the waiter approaching their table with the coffee they had ordered, she moved to arm's length, saying, 'That would be rather foolish on so short an acquaintance, don't you think? Look, the coffee's arrived. Shall we...?'

'If you insist.' His tone was dry.

'And then you can tell me the reason for our meeting tonight and then—'

'We can go home?' he finished silkily, his eyes piercingly intuitive. 'Sorry, Joanne, there's the floor show to go yet; you're stuck with me for a little while longer.'

She smiled, a polite social smile as though she thought he was joking, before turning and walking to their table, his hand on the small of her back seeming to burn her skin through the silk of her dress.

How was it that in just a few hours this man seemed to have established an intimacy that even her closest friends didn't enjoy? she asked herself weakly, sinking down on to her chair with a tiny sigh of relief that she had made it without falling to the floor in a quivering heap. The questions he had asked, the things he had suggested! Her racing thoughts were brought to a stunned halt as she felt his lips on the back of her neck, his mouth warm and vibrant against the creamy softness of her skin, before he seated himself with easy composure in his chair.

'Don't...don't do that.'

'What?' Her voice had been a trembling whisper and he surveyed her with brilliantly blue eyes before asking again, 'Don't do what?'

'You know what.' She glared at him, her temper rising as her senses unfroze.

'Kiss you?' he asked softly. 'Is that so hard to say?'

'It wasn't a kiss, it was...' She couldn't find an appropriate word and he let her flounder for a minute before he said, his voice deep and dark and husky, 'Whatever it was to you, Joanne, to me it was a kiss. Do you mean to say that you don't wear your hair like that to tempt more of the same?'

'What?' She was absolutely lost for words.

'The exposure of that soft, fragrant skin, normally hidden by a curtain of silk that keeps the secret place so private—you don't know what a subtle turn-on that is to the average red-blooded male?' he asked softly as she stared at him blankly. 'It's restraint combined with voluptuousness, lasciviousness with suppression—it's ...sexy, every man's dream of the perfect virginal demure beauty who turns into a seductress in the bedroom.'

'You're mad.' Joanne realised she had been holding her breath as the gravelly male voice had woven a sensual spell which had enclosed the two of them in their own little world. 'I just wore my hair up because it looks better with this dress—'

'Oh, don't spoil it.' He wasn't smiling but the devilish eyes were alight with amusement.

'Now, look.' She took a long, deep, hard breath and

forced herself to get control. This was ridiculous; some-how everything had got out of hand and she wasn't at all sure how it had happened, but one thing she did know was that Hawk Mallen was playing with her like a cat with a mouse. She didn't believe for one moment he was attracted to her—how could a multi-millionaire of the calibre of this one be interested in a little nobody like her? It didn't add up—not for one minute, and she wasn't stupid whatever he thought, and she'd tell him so right now. 'You assured me this afternoon that we were meeting for a purpose, that this wasn't a...'

'Date?' he supplied helpfully.

'Yes.' And if he interrupted her again he'd have a cup of coffee tipped over his head. 'So we've eaten and danced and done the social chit-chat bit, and now I'd really like to know why you have brought me here to-night.'

'You don't think it's because I wanted to know you better, because I'm interested in you?' he asked expressionlessly.

He'd read her mind again, and she had the uneasy feeling he hadn't found it hard to do. Was she really so transparent? she asked herself silently. She didn't think anyone else thought so; in fact, Charles had often praised what he called her 'poker face', which gave nothing away whatever the circumstances.

'Mr Mallen—' she couldn't call him Hawk, she just couldn't '—you could doubtless have your pick of most of London's finest so the answer to that is no.'

'London's finest.' He nodded thoughtfully. 'I see.'

'So?' She forced a smile. 'If you don't mind?'

He stared at her for a good thirty seconds, his blue eyes shadowed and intent as they searched her face, and then he settled back in his seat, stretching slightly before he said, 'Right, down to business. I don't need you at Concise Publications, Joanne—' her heart gave a big leap and then thudded loudly '—but from all I've heard and read and seen I think you would be an asset to the Mallen Corporation. I intend to bring in a new managing director for Concise Publications; I've already approached the man and he's accepted my offer and he'll bring his own publishing assistant with him; they've worked together for years.'

She nodded slowly. So he had never intended to take on the job permanently? She should have guessed, really; Concise Publications was just a tiny little cog in the vast machine of the Mallen empire.

'Are you interested enough for me to continue?' His voice was cool and flat; suddenly he was one hundred per cent remote tycoon and businessman, the wickedly mocking, charming dinner companion having evaporated like the morning mist.

Was she? She stared at him hard, and then nodded again. 'Yes, please,' she said quietly.

The blue eyes flickered, just once, and she would have given the world to know what was going on in that rapier-sharp, ruthless mind.

'Six months ago the Mallen Corporation acquired a publishing house in France, part of Mallen Books; were you aware of this?' She shook her head quickly. 'The undertaking was unusual in that my grandfather had decided to bale the owner out, and if you knew my grandfather you would understand why I say that. He is first and foremost a businessman and age has not mellowed him one iota.'

She caught the thread of affection in his voice which he was trying to hide and looked at him intently.

'The owner was the son of my grandfather's best friend who died some years ago; he actually helped my grandfather financially when they were young, something my grandfather's never forgotten. However, the son has lost thousands, if not tens of thousands, over the last decade through mismanagement and so on, and the firm is a shambles.' The cool voice was scathing. 'My grandfather wanted the family name to continue in honour to his friend; he also decided to keep the son at the helm... Bad mistake.'

He glanced at her now and the blue eyes were as hard as glass. 'The kindest thing you could say about this guy is that he's a Jonah, and that's the information I've relayed to my grandfather. The truth of the matter is that he's been on the take for years; he's the very antithesis of his father. My grandfather is very ill—' Her eyes widened and he nodded slowly. 'Terminal, but I'd appreciate you keeping that to yourself. He doesn't need this bag of worms dumping in his lap, and for some reason his normally acute judgement is faulty where this guy is concerned. He *wants* to believe the best of him; he's all that's left of his old friend.'

'What are you going to do?' she asked quietly. He loved his grandfather very much; try as he might, the cold, clipped voice and expressionless face couldn't hide the look in his eyes, and it touched her. She didn't want it to, but it did.

'I've done it,' he said flatly. 'Pierre is boss in name only now; he's been paid off, and handsomely, and he's quite happy with that. He's got a string of mistresses to support apart from his family and expensive habits; the firm was just an inconvenience to him. But now I want to pull it round, for my grandfather and also his old friend, who was an honourable man. That's where you would come in.'

'Me?' She couldn't think where.

'You've been in publishing since you left university, you have no personal commitments or distractions, and you don't mind working until the job is done. Added to that, Charles tells me your contribution, certainly over the last three or four years, was the one that brought the money in. He'd lost it—the insight, the business intuition—'

'No!' she protested hotly.

'That's what he told me, Joanne,' Hawk said steadily. 'Now, your personnel file tells me you speak French, right?'

'I do, but…well, I'm rusty and—'

'That's no problem.' He dismissed her stumbling voice with an irritable wave of his hand. 'You can easily brush up on that.'

'What exactly are you offering me?' she asked dazedly. In all her wildest dreams—or nightmares—she hadn't expected this. 'Who would I be publishing assistant to?' She knew it was him but she had to ask anyway, and that would be the end of what sounded like the offer of a lifetime in an industry that was known for its dog-eat-dog ruthlessness.

'Publishing assistant?' He stared at her, and then shook his black head slowly, his eyes piercing her through with clear light. 'I'm not offering you a publishing assistant's job, Joanne. I want you to manage the firm for me, turn it around, make it work.'

'Me?' She knew she was repeating herself but this was just not possible; he had to be teasing her in the most cruel way imaginable.

'It would mean giving up your flat and moving to France,' he said quietly, 'and of necessity the position would be on a six-month trial basis. All your expenses would be paid, of course, and you'd have the same salary Pierre did.' He mentioned a figure that made her mouth fall open. 'The firm is already part of Mallen Books and so you wouldn't be completely out on a limb; you'd have a ready-made avenue of contacts and back-up—a security blanket so to speak. But…' He leant forward in his seat, his dark face cold. 'You would have your work cut out to turn the thing round, especially in the present climate. Still interested enough to think about it?'

Joanne looked at him in a daze. She couldn't say a word; she just couldn't.

'If you *are* interested, we can throw a few facts and figures your way and start the ball rolling. I'd like the new manager installed within weeks and as you are as free as a bird there won't be any messy working-of-notice delay. If you're not...' the piercing eyes were holding hers as though in a vice '...then you will be paid twelve months' salary as a gesture of appreciation for all you've done for Charles's firm in the past, and that's the end of it. Well?'

He relaxed back in his seat and grinned, the same devastating, knee-trembling grin as before, his blue gaze washing over her stunned countenance. 'What's it to be, Joanne?'

CHAPTER THREE

'AND he wants your answer tomorrow morning, is that right?' Charles's voice had been sleepy when he'd answered the phone—it was past midnight after all—but once Joanne had begun to talk the telephone had fairly crackled with excitement.

'He wants to know if I'm interested enough to go on to the next phase,' Joanne answered quietly, 'and if I am he'll put me more fully in the picture.'

'And are you?' Charles asked evenly.

'I suppose so, but if I don't make a go of it and I'm left with egg on my face...'

'And if you do make a go of it the world's your oyster,' Charles said steadily. 'Think of it, Joanne; it's a dream of a career move, and frankly it sounds like he's only asking you to do what you've been doing for me for five years. We've worked so closely together there isn't a thing you don't know about managing a publishing house.'

'But this one is so much bigger.' That sounded rude and she added quickly, 'Well, a bit bigger, and it's in France and—'

'You could do it and Hawk Mallen knows it or else he wouldn't have offered you the job.'

'Charles, I'm sorry I phoned you at this time of night, but I don't feel I know enough about the Mallen Corporation and...and Hawk Mallen to make a decision. Would you mind filling me in on what you know?'

'On Hawk or the Mallen empire?' Charles's voice was very dry.

'Both.'

By the time they finished the call, fifteen minutes later, Joanne knew the Mallen Corporation had been founded by Hawk's American/French grandfather over fifty years ago, beginning with a textile warehouse shop that quickly grew into a string of the same and then diversified into more avenues than even Charles was sure of. The old man had had one son, Hawk's father, who, as Hawk had already mentioned, had been killed in an automobile accident, thereupon making Hawk a millionaire several times over at the tender age of twenty.

Charles had said more, much more, but Joanne had found her attention wandering more than once as a pair of very blue, piercingly intent eyes kept swimming into her consciousness. Hawk Mallen was a mesmerising man to be with and the compelling weight of his personality stayed long after the man himself had gone. He exuded energy and power and vigour, and those moments in his arms on the dance-floor... She shut her eyes as her senses swam. If she took this job—*if*—she would make sure she never put herself in such a vulnerable position again.

Her thoughts continued along this same path once the call had ended and she had showered and slipped into bed.

Other women, more worldly, experienced women, might be able to handle a man like Hawk and enjoy the challenge, but he frightened her half to death. She shut her eyes tightly in the warm darkness, her toes curling into the linen covers.

Not that he had behaved as anything but the perfect gentleman on their ride home, seeing her to her door with a polite handshake and almost distant smile that would have sat well on a maiden aunt. In fact from the moment he had explained about the job one could almost have called his attitude cool, certainly formal... She refused to recognise even a shred of pique at his lack of interest. It suited her—the fact that he was concerned only with her ability to do the job he had in mind. *It did*. She knew only too well how the man-woman relationship, with all its complications, could prove a time bomb that ruined the lives of everyone within a mile radius.

As though it were yesterday her mother's face was there, pretty, irritated, as she had handed her over to the social worker at the home. 'It will only be for a little while, Joanne.' Her mother had clearly wished she were anywhere but in the neat, orderly office with officialdom present. 'Just until Mummy gets a nice house to live in.'

The 'nice house' had taken three years to achieve, three years in which she was moved from foster home to foster home, until, at the age of seven, her mother had married. Not again—she had never been married to Joanne's father who had deserted his pregnant girlfriend once the good news was imparted—but for the first time. That marriage had lasted nine months, and by the time she was eight she was back in a foster home again, with the knowledge that her mother could barely wait to see the back of her.

When she was nine her mother had married Bob, and it had been at his insistence that she was once again placed in her mother's care.

She had never wanted to be alone with Bob; she hadn't been able to put it into words at the time—the strange feeling she experienced when his pale, almost opaque eyes slid over her slim, childish body—but when the marriage had been two months old, and the police had arrived on the doorstep one morning, she had known then, young as she was, that she had been right to withstand his overtures of friendship. He had been convicted of several cases of child abuse, a paedophile of the worst kind, and strangely her mother had seemed to blame her for the break-up of her second marriage, screaming at her that she should never have had her back to stay, that if Bob hadn't known about Joanne he wouldn't have asked her to marry him and she would have been spared all the resulting humiliation.

She had been dispatched to the children's home the day after the court case, and had known then that she would never live with her mother again. Her mother had visited her now and again over the next few years, usually with a different 'uncle' in tow each time, some jovial and loud, some not so jolly, but had always managed to make her feel the visit was on sufferance.

The caustic memories of a thousand little rejections which added up to a gigantic whole had burnt so painfully deep within her psyche that even now they made her screw up her eyes and curl into a tight little embryonic ball under the covers.

Commitment, marriage, men—it all meant disappointment and betrayal; she had learnt the fact first-hand, watching her mother's desperate search for love. And children—the biological fruit of that sexual urge which drove men into pretending they were what they weren't, and foolish women into believing it—were the innocent casualties that suffered the most.

She had vowed many times during her tear-filled adolescence that she would never allow herself to be subjugated like her mother; she didn't want or need a man in her life—they meant trouble and pain and ultimately disappointment. Her mother had grown bitter in time— in the last conversation they had had before she died, she had told Joanne over and over again that it wasn't in a man's nature to be monogamous, that marriage and fidelity were the world's biggest lie.

Did she, Joanne, really believe that? she asked herself now, her eyes still tightly shut. She wasn't sure, not deep inside, but she was sure that she would never dare to take the risk, and also that casual relationships, of the sort her mother had eventually subscribed to, were not for her. And whenever the longing to have someone—one man, to come home to, to love—overwhelmed her—as it did more and more as each year ticked by—she drew on the memories and the agony of the past and it fled.

She had her work, her home and her friends—it was safe, controlled, she was in charge and no one could hurt her. It wasn't ideal, but it would have to do.

Charles and Clare had helped her erase some of the pain of the past, as much by the way they lived, their devotion to each other and their children, as their actual friendship. For the first time she had found it within herself to acknowledge that some folk—the lucky ones—could find that elusive element called true love and hang on to it despite all the trials and heartache. But not her. Definitely not her. She just didn't have what it would take. She had made that decision years ago and there was no reason for any doubts now—*none*, not one.

Once Joanne had accepted Hawk Mallen's offer the next day she found herself swept into a kind of whirlwind that had her breathless most of the time. In view of all she had previously decided about the need for a change, for fresh fields and new horizons, the offer was too good to turn down, but she had thought one of his countless minions would deal with her from that point and it was disconcerting to find that Hawk himself intended to oversee each detail. He was the sort of man who generated excitement and flurry and sheer atmosphere wherever he was, and the following weeks sped by in ever increasing velocity.

Of course she could appreciate Bergique & Son's future was close to his heart, or his grandfather's, to be more precise, and he needed to keep a tight hold of the reins, but the apprehension and unease she had felt that first night was always there, at the back of her mind. And she couldn't quite work out why. He was business-like, cool, remote, but not unhelpful—very much the austere, detached tycoon, but always ready to listen to her ideas or opinions. And yet... 'Oh, stop imagining things.' She leant against the wall of the lift which was whisking her up to the meeting with Hawk that morning.

Just because she had caught him looking at her...oddly once or twice, it didn't mean he was regretting his decision to appoint her manageress of the failing firm, or that he was going to tell her he had changed his mind, or any of the other scenarios she had gone through each night in the quiet of her bed.

He was just a disturbing man, that was all it was, and in a few more days she would be over the Channel in France and he would be here in England, or dashing off to America or any one of a dozen countries he seemed to visit frequently. She just had to be cool, calm and collected, serene even, in the five days that were left. That wasn't beyond her, surely?

It shouldn't have been. It probably *wouldn't* have been, if poor Maggie, who had been totally overawed by Hawk's commanding presence from day one, hadn't tripped over her own feet and deposited most of their morning coffee right over her illustrious boss's immaculate silk-covered chest.

As the burning liquid hit his torso Hawk swore—once but very thoroughly—leaping up from his chair like a scalded cat—and scalded he certainly was. The bedlam was immediate, Maggie's horrified apology cut short as she burst into tears, several people from the outer office cannoning into the room at the sound of Hawk's yell, the telephone choosing that moment to begin ringing and all the papers on Hawk's desk tumbling to the floor as Joanne jumped up to help and knocked them with her arm.

'Quiet!' The thirty-second mayhem stopped as suddenly as it had begun as Hawk roared the order into the chaos, the only sound breaking the dead silence that followed being Maggie's muted wailing and the continuing ring of the telephone. 'Please, I'm fine, no harm done—get Maggie a cup of tea or whatever else you keep out there for emergencies,' Hawk fired in a staccato burst that told Joanne he was very definitely not all right. 'And someone answer that damn phone!'

As the others filed out, taking the weeping Maggie with them, Hawk shut the door behind them, wincing slightly as he did so, before peeling his steaming shirt out of the flat waistband of his trousers, discarding his tie and beginning to undo the buttons.

'What are you doing?' It was a squeak.

'What do you think I'm doing?' He clearly wasn't in the mood for rhetorical questions and she really couldn't blame him, but neither could she quite believe he was going to strip half naked in the office in the middle of a working day. He was, and apparently with a complete disregard for modesty that left her breathless. Only it wasn't just his lack of propriety that was causing the blood to race through every nerve and sinew.

Clothed, Hawk Mallen had the sort of lean, athletic physique that made the female heart beat a little faster; *half* clothed, the dark power radiated from him in tangible waves, impossible to ignore. Not that Joanne made any attempt to ignore it—she looked; she couldn't help it.

'Joanne?'

It was humiliating to realise he had spoken her name twice before it registered on her dazed senses, but the big broad shoulders and hairy, muscled chest had her knees ready to buckle under her. Useless to tell herself she was pathetic, ridiculous—a female voyeur; he was affecting her in a way no other man had ever done before and in a way she wouldn't have dreamed possible even moments before. He was…well, he was… She dragged her eyes up to the piercing blue gaze which was waiting for her.

'I asked you if you would get someone to pop to Harrods and pick up a shirt,' he said softly, his lips quirking with amusement. 'It's nearer than my hotel and I have an account there; they'll know what to send.'

He knew! He knew the thoughts that had shocked her with their lasciviousness and he was laughing at her.

Her head shot up, her honey-brown eyes darkening as the knowledge provided a welcome shot of adrenalin. 'Of course.' Her voice was taut and she kept her eyes strictly on his face, but the tanned expanse beneath them was still there.

'And perhaps you'd dispose of this?' He handed her the damp shirt, the muscles in his chest flexing as he did so. 'I'm going to hose myself down in Charles's washroom; I can feel that damn coffee's still burning my skin.'

She took the shirt as though it were going to bite her, knowing her face was flooded with colour but unable to do anything about it. He'd done this on purpose—oh, not the coffee, she couldn't blame that on him, but this…this *flaunting* of himself, she thought balefully. To embarrass her, to show her he was as unconcerned about her seeing him in a state of undress as…as the office furniture! It was added confirmation, as if she needed any, that she was just a working machine to him, little more than a number—

'Joanne?' The dark voice was patient. 'Harrods?'

'Oh, yes—yes, of course.' She shot out of the office as though the devil himself was after her, and in a way she felt that he was.

How could she have ogled him like that? she thought miserably after she'd sent one of the office staff darting off to Harrods. She'd all but licked her lips! What must he have thought? That she was attracted to him? Worse, that she was letting him *know* that she was attracted to him? She'd die if he'd thought that—she would; she'd just die—

'Joanne?' Maggie's woebegone voice cut into her painful introspection. 'How mad is he—Mr Mallen? I can't believe I did that.'

You and me both, Joanne thought as the mortification burnt deep. 'He's all right; don't worry.' She forced her voice to sound bright and matter-of-fact. 'Worse things happen at sea and all that.'

'I wish I was at sea; I wish I was anywhere but here,' Maggie said flatly. 'I don't know what it is about him but he makes me all fingers and thumbs; do you know what I mean?'

I do; oh, I do. 'He's only here for another three weeks—' Joanne smiled briskly into Maggie's puppy-dog eyes '—and then Mr Brigmore's replacement will be at the helm. Just…just treat him like you would Mr Brigmore till then, Maggie.'

'Just treat him like you would Mr Brigmore'. The absurdity of the statement hit her full between the eyes a little while later when she took the neatly packaged silk shirt in to Hawk. She hadn't ventured back into his office in the meantime—she knew her limitations and sitting opposite a half-naked Hawk Mallen discussing business matters was one of them—and her knock at his door was tentative in the extreme.

He was sitting at his desk as she entered, apparently engrossed in the papers in front of him, but as he raised an expressionless face to her, his startling blue eyes hooded and cool, she knew, she just *knew*, he was fully aware of the impact his raw, vigorous brand of masculinity had on the opposite sex.

'Your shirt.' She wanted to fling the thing on his desk

and run but she forced herself to smile politely and hand it to him without undue haste.

'Thanks.' He smiled, and her heart jerked and then flew round her chest like a caged bird. 'I presume poor Maggie is still covered with confusion?' he said quietly as he undid the Cellophane, shaking the beautiful grey silk shirt free of creases. 'Was she like that with Charles? So jumpy all the time?'

With Charles? Was he joking? She looked straight into the tanned face and saw he was perfectly serious.

'No, not really,' she said carefully.

'But I make her nervous.' His eyes were intent on hers as he pulled the silk over muscled skin and she forced herself not to swallow, although agitation had created a lump in her throat the size of a golf ball. 'Why is that? Is she worried she might lose her job?'

Oh, get a move on, for goodness' sake. He had stood up to pull on the shirt and now he moved round in front of his desk, perching on the edge of it as he began to fasten the buttons from the bottom up. There was something so intimate, so ridiculously intimate in the action that funny little sensations seemed to be going off in every part of her body, her skin hot and flushed and her mouth dry.

'Her job?' Her voice sounded vague even to herself and she forced it down a decibel as she said, 'No, I don't think so; she just isn't very good with new people at first.'

'I see.' The blue eyes narrowed and he leant forward, the last three or four buttons still undone and revealing far more dark curling body hair than was good for her pulse rate. 'And you?' he asked softly. 'What about you?'

'Me?' The squeak was back.

'Have I won you over by my decorous behaviour over the last few weeks?' he asked with wicked ease, his eyes almost silver as they moved over the rich curtain of silky red hair and down to her eyes again. 'Or am I still the monster from hell bent on destruction and ruination?'

'I didn't say that,' she protested quickly.

'You didn't have to.' The deep husky voice with its unusual gravelly texture was self-deprecating. 'I've seen dislike and fear in eyes far more adept at hiding it than yours. Besides—' he leant back again, the movement bringing hard-muscled thighs into play '—I seem to remember you accused me of throwing poor Charles out on his ear? And ''poor Charles'' was your terminology, not mine, incidentally,' he added drily.

'I've said I was sorry about that.' She looked at him steadily.

'And it's very bad manners to bring it up again?' He added the bit she hadn't dared to say. 'But then I'm not a true-blue Englishman, am I, Joanne?' he said silkily. 'My paternal grandparents were of American and French extraction, and my father married a beautiful Italian countess, so that makes me a…mongrel?'

A mongrel? There was no mongrel ever born who looked like Hawk Mallen. But the Italian bit explained his dark good looks, she thought silently, and the jet-black hair that was such a devastating contrast to the brilliant blue eyes. The eyes must be from his father's side… She checked her thoughts and said hastily, 'I hardly think a mongrel.'

'No?' He grinned at her, his teeth white in the tanned skin of his face. 'Well, perhaps not,' he conceded sardonically. 'I would certainly kill any man who suggested so.'

'I don't doubt it.' And she meant it.

'But you haven't answered my question, tactful Joanne,' he drawled mockingly.

'What question?' She wanted to whirl round and run, turn the clock back an hour to the state of play that had existed before the wretched coffee, before this broodingly dangerous being had emerged from the tycoon's skin; but it was too late.

'Have I persuaded you that I am a normal nice man?' he asked drily. 'Or is this outside the realms of possibility?'

'I don't know what you want me to say.' She stared at him, her golden eyes enormous. 'I work for you—'

'Forget the working for me.' It was sharp, too sharp, and as he saw her flinch he moderated his tone, his eyes continuing to gleam like molten silver as he said, 'Tell me the truth, Joanne, that's all I ask.'

That was never all a man like him asked, she thought faintly, but if he wanted the truth then he could have it, job or no job.

'I don't think "normal" and the name Mallen are compatible,' she said quietly. 'From what I've heard about your grandfather he is out of the ordinary too. As for nice—well, I don't know you, do I?' she prevaricated uneasily. 'You might be.'

'But you doubt it.'

She had expected him to be angry but the hard mouth was twitching with amusement.

'You are right about my grandfather, Joanne,' he said thoughtfully after a few moments of holding her with the mesmerising power of his eyes. 'He is a character, quite a character. Ruthless, irascible, probably the most impatient man I've ever met—'

'But with a heart of gold?' she put in daringly before she could stop herself.

The quirk to his lips acknowledged her bravery. 'No, he is as hard as iron.' All amusement fled as he added, 'He's had to be; if you knew his life story you would understand that. He was born poor, dirt-poor, and when he first met my grandmother he told her he wouldn't marry her until he had made his first million. She was

from a rich French family, you see, and people said...
Well, you can imagine what they said,' he added flatly.

'She waited ten years for him and they had two years
together, as man and wife, before my father was born.
She died having him.' Her shock was evident and he
shook his head slowly as he said, 'He never looked at
another woman after she died and he's had offers—
plenty. My father was the image of her, apparently, but
strangely they never got on. It caused the old man a lot
of grief, especially after my parents were killed, although
he's never discussed it.'

'But he has you, his grandson.'

'Yes, he has me,' he agreed softly.

'And that's more family than some people have.' She
hadn't meant to vocalise that thought, it had just popped
out of its own volition, and now she flushed scarlet as
she lowered her eyes and aimed to bring the conversation back on a more mundane level. 'That financial statement you had from Pierre—I think—'

'Why are you so frightened of me, Joanne?' he asked
quietly.

'What?'

As she raised her eyes again he levered himself off
the desk, bringing his lean, lithe body to within inches
of her own and noting the little backward step that she
made before checking herself with a tightening of his
mouth.

'You find me threatening, is that it?' He moved an
inch or so closer and this time she forced herself to stand
absolutely still, her small chin rising a notch as she
stared steadily into the glittering eyes. 'An alien in the
safe little world you have created for yourself?'

It was so near the mark that her breath caught in her
throat for a moment, his subtle menace more pronounced
as he came close enough for the wickedly blended, sensual aftershave he wore to stroke her senses, heightening

her awareness of him so it became painful. She had to stop this, had to defuse things…

'I work for you, that's all—'

'Perhaps I don't want that to be all,' he said silkily.

Her eyes were locked with his, her limbs frozen, even as her brain was telling her to get out, to remove herself from the line of fire. His height was forcing her head to tilt back as she stared up at him and she was vitally aware of the muscled breadth of him, of the power of that magnificent chest cage she had so recently seen in all its splendour.

'What about you, Joanne?' His voice was warm and deep, caressing her as expertly as though he were touching her. 'What do you want?'

She wanted to tell him she wasn't interested, that he had to leave her alone, that he was the last man, the very last man, she would get involved with, but somehow all she could do was stare at him, quite unable to move or speak.

'You are…tantalising, do you know that?' he asked huskily. 'A delicious blend of grown-up woman and young girl contained in a creamy soft skin that makes me want to bite it—gently of course,' he added softly as her eyes widened. 'And that dusting of freckles across your nose—I didn't know women still had freckles. Come out with me tonight, to a show or something.'

'What?' The last bit was so abrupt she didn't know if she had heard right.

'A show. With me. Tonight.' It was said mockingly, but there was a note in the dark voice that made her toes curl, and it was this, more than anything, that flashed a red warning light in front of her vision.

'I don't think so.' She tried for cool firmness and failed miserably. 'I've always held the belief that work and play should be quite separate,' she said primly, avoiding his eyes.

'So have I,' he agreed immediately.

'Well, then.'

'But there always has to be one exception to the rule, besides which within days you won't be around for it to matter much, one way or the other,' he said smoothly.

So this was going to be a wham, bam, thank-you-ma'am kind of evening? she thought numbly. What was he expecting? Payment in kind for the marvellous job offer? Was that it? And then she could scoot off across the Channel, no doubt forgotten the moment her bag was packed?

'Joanne?' He took her shoulders in his hands, his touch jerking her head—which had been drooping forward—up to meet the ice-blue gaze. 'I'm suggesting an evening out, just that, okay? I have never yet used my position to blackmail a woman into my bed and I have no intention of starting with you.'

He'd done it again—read her mind, she thought frantically.

'And while we're on the subject you got the job on merit, pure and simple, just in case that fertile little imagination of yours has decided otherwise.' He was mad; that much was obvious from the frosty countenance surveying her.

'I didn't think—'

'And don't lie to me.' The black brows frowned at her. 'I told you before, I expect the truth.'

He was still holding her, her eyes on a level with his tanned throat, and whether it was the fact that her heart was pounding like a sledgehammer, which was humiliating in itself, or that whatever the situation he always seemed to put *her* in the wrong, she didn't know, but suddenly she found herself saying, 'All right, I did think you were proposing more than a show if you want to know, and frankly that wouldn't be too unusual in this day and age with most of the men I know,' she finished caustically.

'Then perhaps it's time to get to know a different sort of man,' he said silkily. 'One that can think with his brain rather than a lower part of his anatomy.'

'Like you, you mean?' she flashed back hotly.

'Why all this anger and resentment?' He had changed. In an instant the derisive cutting element had gone and the sensuously persuasive and much more dangerous Hawk was back, his eyes almost stroking her hot skin as they wandered over her flushed face. 'Is it such a crime to want to spend an evening in your company, Joanne? In spite of all the formidable keep-off signs you must have the occasional brave man dare to make such a suggestion?'

She shrugged, moving away from him as she did so, and he made no effort to stop her. 'I don't have much time for socialising,' she said briefly, feeling a little better when there were a few feet of air between them.

'So your idea of keeping work and play separate boils down to all work and no play?' he asked mockingly. 'What an industrious little worker I have in my midst.'

'I would have thought you'd be pleased,' she said tightly, refusing to be drawn.

'So would I.' He stared at her for a moment, his voice thoughtful. 'Yes, so would I. My loss of a theatre companion is Bergique & Son's gain after all. Well, it will have to be lunch, then—nice tame lunch in a busy crowded restaurant where you will be quite safe from my wicked intentions.'

She glared at him, she couldn't help it, but he seemed oblivious to her fury, turning to pick up the tie which had arrived with the shirt and walking round to the other side of the desk again as he said, 'Be ready at twelve.'

'But—'

'And order some more coffee, would you? Preferably

delivered by anyone other than Maggie,' he added drily, his eyes on his desk.

Immediately it was all business mode again, the rapier, sharp mind she had come to respect and admire over the last few weeks homed in on the financial report from Pierre Bergique they had been about to discuss when Maggie had committed her prize *faux pas*.

She had never met anyone who could metamorphose so completely, she thought testily, passing on the request for coffee before reseating herself opposite the big dark figure behind the desk. He couldn't have any real feelings at all; it seemed as though he was made of granite, hard, unyielding granite, with just a covering of flesh and skin on the outside. But what an outside...

The brilliant blue eyes suddenly rose and focused on her face and she felt their impact like a bolt of lightning. 'Relax, Joanne,' he said easily. 'You're no good to me all tensed up and ready to strike; I want your full attention on this report.'

'I beg your pardon—?'

'You were thinking of excuses to get out of lunch.' The cool voice was irritatingly sure of itself but she didn't dissuade him; she would far rather he think her lack of concentration was due to what he had suggested rather than her musing on his magnificent body. 'Rest assured there isn't one, so let's press on with the matter in hand.'

'I'm more than ready to do what you want.' It was an unfortunate choice of words, and the haughty expression with which she had spoken the clipped declaration faltered as his black eyebrows rose.

'I wish.' Two words, and his head had already lowered to the papers in front of him, but the shivers of sensation continued to flow up and down her spine for a few minutes more, making the full attention he had requested impossible.

*   *   *

The sky was overcast and there was a slight drizzle in the air as they walked out of the building at three minutes past twelve, the cold October day making the warmth of summer a distant memory. Hawk's car was crouching in its reserved space next to her little red Fiesta, and never had 'his' and 'hers' been so markedly different.

The thought brought a little smile to her lips as Hawk opened the passenger door for her and she slid inside the luxuriously plush interior, and he paused before moving round the car, peering in the open door as he said, 'What?'

'What?' She arched her brows at him although she knew exactly what he had meant.

'Why the smile? You don't often smile in my company,' he added sardonically.

'It was nothing, just the cars. It just struck me yours looks as though it could eat mine for breakfast,' she said lightly.

'If you work the miracle with Bergique & Son you'll be able to treat yourself to anything you fancy.' There was a note to his voice she couldn't quite place.

'I'm quite content with my little Fiesta,' she said quietly.

'Are you, Joanne? Quite content, that is?'

They both knew he wasn't referring to her choice of car, and she stared up into the dark, handsome face above her, forcing her eyes not to fall from his and her features to betray none of her inner turmoil as she said, 'Perfectly. It's never let me down yet, besides which I wouldn't feel comfortable driving anything too flash.'

'Flash?'

She had nettled him and it felt wonderfully good. 'My Fiesta is ideal for nipping in and out of London traffic,' she continued sweetly, 'and I can park it almost any-where.'

He eyed her darkly for one moment before shutting the passenger door very quietly, and as he slid into the driving seat a few seconds later she had the brief satisfaction of knowing she had held her own for once.

There were several good restaurants within easy reach but after they had been driving for some fifteen minutes, the powerful car growling with impatience at the lunchtime traffic, she asked the question that had been hovering on her lips for the last few miles. 'Where are we going?'

'I've an appointment before we eat; you don't mind?' he said absently, his eyes on the road ahead. 'It won't take long.'

'No, of course not.'

He didn't elaborate further and she didn't like to ask, but when, nearly half an hour later, they still hadn't arrived and the concrete jungle had given way to an altogether more pleasant residential aspect, she was just on the verge of nerving herself to enquire as to the exact location of their destination when Hawk drew off the wide, tree-lined street and on to what was virtually a private road. 'Hawk? Where—?'

'Hang on a moment.' As she'd spoken a pair of massive wooden gates, which wouldn't have been out of place in a bank, had appeared in front of them, set in an eight-foot-high brick wall that was formidable. As the driver's window wound down he inserted a small key into a little box and immediately the gates glided open, revealing a long winding drive threading through beautifully landscaped grounds.

'Who lives here?' she asked nervously, her eyes turning to the hard dark profile as the powerful car moved smoothly forward.

'A business colleague.' If he heard the note of panic in her voice he didn't comment. 'He's emigrating to Canada shortly and has given me first option on the house before he puts it on the open market. He's taken his family to Bermuda for a few days so suggested I might like to browse round and make up my mind for when he returns. He's due back tomorrow but it's been one hell of a week and this is the first opportunity I've had to call by.'

'You're thinking of buying a house in England?' she asked faintly. She knew he had a mansion of a place in the States, Beverly Hills, no less, as well as a bachelor pad in New York—the office grapevine had been full of it—but why England? He had told her he had no intention of overseeing Concise Publications any longer than it took for Charles's replacement to settle in, but then, the Mallen Corporation was huge. Obviously they had far bigger fish to fry in London than Charles's operation, so why not a home here? She knew he hated the anonymity of hotels; he had been nothing if not vocal about the subject for weeks.

'Maybe.' The blue gaze flashed over her worried face and shining red hair before returning to the windscreen. 'Maybe not. I loathe hotels, that much is common knowledge, but in the States and Italy I've got my own places—' the office gossip missed the one in Italy, Joanne thought wryly '—and I usually stay with a friend when I'm in Germany. Other countries normally only necessitate a brief visit.'

Friend of the female gender? She was surprised at how much the thought hurt. No, not hurt, she corrected quickly in her mind, her face flaming as though she had voiced it. Irritated, annoyed, that was all, and only then because she hated the thought of any man clicking his fingers and women falling into line, be they Germans, Italians, or little pink Martians with blue spots.

'Hmm, impressive.'

His voice focused her eyes on the imposing residence at the end of the drive, and she had to agree with him—

it was impressive all right. The house was three storeys tall, liberally covered in red and green ivy with myriad windows and the sort of front door that would grace any stately home. It was huge, splendid, the sort of place that would take a small army to run and maintain it, and Joanne hated it on sight.

It didn't improve on further acquaintance. The interior was larger than life, the last word in elegance, but Joanne couldn't believe that real flesh-and-blood people lived in such a dignified, coldly perfect mausoleum of a place—especially children.

She said little as they were shown round by a young attractive housekeeper who looked as though she did modelling in her spare time, but then neither did Hawk, beyond refusing refreshments at the end of the tour and ushering her out to the car with the minimum of good-byes.

'Well?' They stood at the bottom of the curved stone steps, looking out across the vast expanse of bowling-green-smooth lawn surrounded by massive oaks. 'What did you think?' he asked expressionlessly. 'Some kind of edifice, eh?' His American accent was suddenly much stronger—she normally barely noticed it—and she paused for a moment before answering.

Should she prevaricate, humour him? she thought flatly. All Americans loved stately homes—it was an appreciation given to them along with their mother's milk—and this home was certainly stately. If he intended to buy it, and she told him what she really thought, he wasn't going to be very pleased. But he *had* asked. And he had a mania for the truth...

'It's certainly that.' She paused again. 'But...'

'But?' he asked coolly.

'I'm sorry, it's beautiful, but as a home it just wouldn't be my cup of tea,' she said colloquially.

'There's no warmth, no real feel about it. I'm sorry,' she added again when he still didn't speak.

'You're a roses round the door girl?' The tone was cynical in the extreme, and immediately her hackles rose.

'Probably.' And she was damned if she was going to apologise for the fact to him.

'A cottage in the country, with resident cat, dog and pigeons, not to mention a couple of fat healthy babies thrown in?' he continued derisively.

She felt her temper rise but didn't even try to hold on to it. 'If I ever got married, and frankly that's not on my agenda, I'd much prefer what you've just described than that...that so-called edifice,' she bit back heatedly. 'And if you're insinuating that makes me naive, so be it. Money isn't everything, you know. Just because you've been born with a silver cutlery set, let alone a spoon, it doesn't make you an authority on what other people should like.'

'Indeed it doesn't,' he said gravely.

'And considering you're always belly-aching about the truth you shouldn't object when you get just that,' she continued hotly.

'Belly-aching?'

'Added to which I didn't ask to come and look at your wretched house; in fact I didn't have any say in the matter—something which is not unusual with you!'

'Joanne, I don't *like* the house—'

'And you might be a multi-millionaire with the power to scare people half to death, like poor Maggie, but you function just the same as everyone else, Hawk Mallen, at root level—the same bodily needs, the same requirement to bathe, to eat, to go to the loo—'

'Please, don't go on; delicacy forbids it.'

'And don't *laugh* at me!'

When, in the next moment, she was pulled into his

arms and his mouth descended in a kiss that was all fire and sensation, she never even thought about struggling. As her head began to spin she felt herself folded even more securely against the hard bulk of him, the kiss becoming warm, sensuous, coaxing, turning her legs to jelly and her limbs fluid. That delicious fragrance, peculiar to him, was all about her, fuelling the need, adding another dimension to the sexual fever that had flared so suddenly she couldn't fight it.

His mouth was experienced, his tongue exploring, and the ripples of desire that were flooding every part of her body far too sweet to deny.

The cold October afternoon, all the warnings she had given herself for weeks, the fact that this was Hawk Mallen—*Hawk Mallen*—weren't real any more. All that was real was this world of light and pleasure and sheer sensation behind her closed eyelids, a world she hadn't known existed, hadn't imagined in her wildest dreams.

And then it stopped. His head lifted from hers, his arms released her, and his voice, controlled, tight even, spoke as matter-of-factly as though they had been discussing the weather. 'Lunch, I think?'

CHAPTER FOUR

SHE must have been mad, quite, quite mad. Oh, *Joanne*... She ground her teeth in frustration, twisting violently in the bed, which was already a heap of tangled covers, before flinging herself jerkily to the edge and sitting up in one irritable, furious movement. How could she, how *could* she have let Hawk Mallen dominate her senses so completely earlier that day, after all the warnings she had given herself for weeks?

That first evening, back in September, she had made a cast-iron resolution never to become vulnerable around him, never to let her defences down, to maintain a distance at all costs. And she had kept it through all the following weeks of working together; she had been calm, efficient, in control. Or, at least, she had *thought* she was in control.

The notion that Hawk had allowed her to think that way while he had been quietly biding his time had her eyes narrowing in a face that was already flushed and cross. It hadn't been difficult to maintain a distance over the last few weeks, if she thought about it, because Hawk himself had been the same. What had been his idea? Lulling her into a false sense of security before he struck?

She shook her head bewilderedly as she rose from the bed, slipping her thick, cosy towelling robe over her nightie before wandering over to the window and gazing out over the sleeping night, the darkness dotted here and there by the odd light, which showed there were other night owls who couldn't sleep.

She had to be careful not to let her imagination run

away with her here. Okay, he had let her know he found
her interesting enough to suggest an evening out at the
theatre, but he had known, like her, that if she accepted
it would of necessity be a one-off before she left for
France, and very probably he had been at a loose end
and had thought she would fill a convenient slot. And
the kiss at lunchtime? Well, he'd made it very clear how
he'd considered that! Her cheeks burnt and she yanked
the belt of the robe more tightly round her slim waist.

It hadn't touched him at all; in fact once he had released her he had dismissed the moments when she had
been in his arms without so much as a word, walking
over to the car and opening the passenger door with an
air of— What? she asked herself wearily. Coldness?
Indifference? Self-assuredness? And she had noticed that
all through lunch and the rest of the afternoon back at
the office he had been very careful not to have any physical contact of even the most platonic kind.

'Not that I wanted any.' She spoke the words out loud
with a kind of defiance, her arms crossed over her middle and her hands clutching her waist. 'I can do without
any come-on from Hawk Mallen; in fact that's the *last*
thing I want.'

The realisation that she was talking to herself dawned
as she heard the hollow note in her words, and she shut
her eyes tight for an infinitesimal moment before stalk-
ing into the kitchen and fixing herself a cup of hot milk,
intensely irritated with both herself and Hawk. She
didn't need this, she really didn't—post-mortems on past
conversations were bad enough at the best of times and
two o'clock in the morning was most definitely *not* the
best of times, not with a busy day looming in front of
her and a desk full of urgent correspondence.

No doubt Hawk was fast asleep. She gulped a mouthful of hot milk so fast it burnt her throat. Oh, blow him,

blow Mallen Books, France, Bergique & Son... everything.

She finished the milk, snuggled down in bed, blanking her mind of everything but the warm comfort of the electric blanket without and the hot sweet milk within. It was a trick she'd learnt in the blackest days of her childhood, and although it was harder than normal tonight to prevent thoughts from intruding she managed it—just—slipping into a troubled slumber populated by cloudy dreams as soon as she pulled the covers up round her ears and shut her eyes.

'All ready for tomorrow?'

'I think so.' Joanne tried to keep all trace of nervousness out of her voice as she answered Hawk's expressionless enquiry. 'I was going to ask you for the tickets and so on, actually; I've been meaning to for days but it's been so hectic...' The last few days since their lunchtime date had passed in a whirl.

'Don't worry, it's all in hand. I'll bring them along tomorrow morning when I pick you up.' He had raised his head from the papers on his desk as he had spoken, his voice steady, and as the piercing eyes met hers she knew he knew how she would react to his words.

'There's no need for you to pick me up.' In spite of the knowledge she was confirming his expectations she couldn't say anything else. 'I've already ordered a taxi,' she continued uncomfortably, 'but thanks for the offer anyway.'

'Cancel it.' His eyes returned to the file at his fingers as though the matter was finished.

'I don't think—'

'Cancel it, Joanne.' It was said in the tone he used when he considered she was being tiresome, and it never failed to grate unbearably. 'It makes far more sense for us to travel together with our destination being the same.' His eyes met hers again.

'You're flying somewhere tomorrow?' she asked in surprise, and then, as the level gaze continued to hold hers and an awful suspicion washed over her, she added weakly, 'Where to?'

'You didn't really think I would throw you in the deep end without a float, did you?' he asked quietly, the dark, husky voice sending tiny little shivers down her spine. 'I'm coming over with you to introduce you to the staff and get things off on the right foot. I shall stay the night, maybe two. Is that all right?' he added with a touch of sardonic wryness that told her her face was speaking her mind.

'There's no need, really,' she said firmly.

'There's every need.'

She looked hard into the enigmatic face in front of her, wondering exactly what was going on in that ruthless mind. 'I'm not overawed by any of this, Hawk,' she said tightly.

'Whether you are or whether you aren't is of no account; I want the French workforce to know that I'm backing the new management one hundred per cent and that they'll toe the line or else.' There was a touch of grimness to the cool voice now. 'People are people the world over, Joanne, and from what I can make out Pierre let his staff get away with murder, simply because he wasn't bothered one way or the other beyond feathering his own nest. You'll meet opposition, covert maybe and perhaps not so covert, but I want to minimise it as far as I can.'

'I can deal with it—'

'Trust me, Joanne.' Blue eyes held honey-brown with a power that was unbreakable. 'I know what I'm talking about.'

'I don't doubt that,' she said primly.

'Yes, you do.' He smiled, his lips twisting wryly. 'You were trying to determine if I had an ulterior motive for accompanying you across the Channel, weren't you?'

It was a challenge, and if she had learnt one thing with this fierce, strange individual it was that you didn't duck and dive.

'Yes.' She stared straight at him, her smooth skin flushing slightly. 'I was. *Have* you?'

'That's what makes you so good at your job, Joanne,' he murmured drily. 'You have no hesitation in going straight for the jugular if you feel right is on your side.'

'You haven't answered my question,' she said steadily.

'That's right, I haven't.' He smiled again, and his eyes were burning into hers.

'And you don't intend to?'

'Right again.' As she opened her mouth to protest he stood up, moving round the desk and to her side with cat-like swiftness. 'You are such a mass of contradictions, aren't you?' he said with a softness that took her fury away and reduced her to a quivering jelly inside. 'So fierce, so straight, at times, and other times as nervous as a little fawn.'

'I hardly think so.' She tried for a sophisticated coolness and failed miserably.

'Your eyes are the colour of a baby deer in its first year, do you know that?' he continued huskily. 'A sun-kissed golden-brown and velvety soft—eyes a man could drown in.'

'And yours have the sharpness of the sea under an icy winter sky, crystal-clear and bitingly cold.' It wasn't meant to be complimentary but he considered her words with his head slightly tilted, those same eyes of which she had spoken laughing at her.

'I quite like that analogy,' he murmured softly. 'It

wouldn't do for an individual bearing the Mallen name
to have puppy-dog eyes.'

Don't let it happen again, Joanne; be strong, be strong.
The voice in her head was savage. Look how you felt
last time when he was soft persuasion one minute and
as distant as the man in the moon the next.

She didn't want her confusion to show, but her sur-
reptitious nip on her bottom lip was caught by the blue
gaze, and after one second more he turned from her, his
eyes hooded.

'I will pick you up at nine in the morning, Joanne.'
His voice was reasonable, even, the sort of voice one
used when discussing somewhat boring arrangements.
'On the dot.'

'All right...thank you.' The gratitude was grudging
but she couldn't help it. She had been nervous enough
about the following day before she knew Hawk was going to accompany her, but now... She forced the panic
which was gripping her throat to subside with sheer will-
power. Everything he had said was reasonable, practical;
she knew that if she considered it rationally. His ap-
proving presence would give her an edge with the staff
she could well do with in the circumstances; it was just
that... Rationality didn't seem to have any place in her
feelings about Hawk Mallen.

She glanced at him now as he sat down in the enormous leather chair which had always seemed to swallow
Charles but fitted Hawk's powerful body perfectly. A
shaft of sunlight from the cold but sunny October day
outside was glancing through the window on to his
cropped head, turning the short hair blue-black, and
somehow the bent head was terribly appealing. She
wanted to run her fingers through that springy, virile
hair, just once, to see what it felt like; she wanted—

She caught her thoughts with something akin to horror, desperately relieved he hadn't looked up as she had

stared at him. The sooner she got to France, settled in, and Hawk left, the better.

Joanne was painfully touched, later that afternoon, by the serious and emotional send-off she received from the office staff. Along with a host of cards, an expensive set of brand-new luggage and copious hugs and kisses, Maggie took her to one side and presented her with an exquisite little crystal clock, tiny but beautifully made. 'It's from me, just me,' the young junior said earnestly, her brown eyes liquid with tears. 'You've been so good to me, Joanne, especially when I first started and was so petrified; I can never thank you enough. I shall miss you like anything.'

'Oh, Maggie.' It was too much, and as Joanne began to cry Maggie joined her, and as the two of them hugged Joanne felt a moment of utter desolation.

'Here.' When she was firmly, but kindly, parted from Maggie, and a balloon glass with a hefty measure of brandy was put in her hand, she recognised Hawk's voice but was unable to see him through the streaming tears. 'Drink it, all of it, and then we'll open the champagne,' he murmured quietly in her ear, before raising his voice to the assembled staff and saying, 'Champagne, everyone, to celebrate Joanne's departure to brighter and better things. And there's a cold buffet laid on; the caterers are on their way up, so clear some tables, okay?'

The resulting bustle and chatter gave Joanne a much needed chance to compose herself, although when she saw the sumptuous spread which Hawk had laid on, along with the bottles of very good vintage champagne, she nearly succumbed to the flood of emotion again. 'You...you shouldn't have gone to so much trouble,' she said weakly after all the appropriate toasts had been made and everyone was in little groups, plates and glasses in hand, talking animatedly. 'I didn't expect anything...'

'Perhaps that's why I did it,' Hawk said softly. They were standing slightly apart from the merry throng, Hawk having insisted on filling her plate for her and standing over her while she tried to force some food past the huge lump in her throat. 'Besides which, everyone thinks one hell of a lot of you, Joanne. I might have had a mutiny on my hands if we hadn't lashed out a bit.'

She glanced up at him, her gaze still luminous with the tears she was holding at bay, and as he stared down into the huge honey-brown orbs the wry smile on his face faded, and their eyes locked and held for endless moments.

'Joanne—?' He stopped abruptly, and his voice was husky as he continued, 'You know they don't want you to go?'

'Don't they?' She wasn't sure if he was talking about the office staff or if his words held a deeper meaning, and she was terrified of the possibility of the latter even as she longed for it with an intensity that shocked her.

'They'll miss you; things won't be the same...' His voice was deep and gravelly, the words seeming to be dragged up from the depths of him, and almost in the same instant he turned from her with a savage movement that spoke of escape and said, 'More champagne?'

She stood quite still as she watched him cross the room and pour a stream of the golden sparkly liquid into one of the large fluted glasses, her senses reeling. She hadn't imagined the raging desire in his eyes when he had looked at her—she hadn't—but there had been something else too, something...dark. She shivered suddenly, in spite of the perfectly regulated temperature within the building. What on earth had happened in his life to make him look like that? she asked herself weakly, but in the next second she was surrounded by a loud, laughing group who drew her into their midst, forcing her to push her agitation to the back of her mind.

When Hawk joined them, just a moment or two later, he handed her the glass of champagne with a smile and a nod, his face cool and distant and the big body slightly aloof. The brief baring of his soul had gone, to be replaced by the ice man who was in perfect control of himself and those about him—benevolent host, gracious conversationalist, but definitely, overwhelmingly untouchable.

CHAPTER FIVE

THE combination of a glass of brandy, two of champagne, and a long day full of emotional turmoil, added to the fact that Joanne had slept badly for the last few nights, ensured that she was asleep as soon as her head touched the pillow that night.

When her neat little bedside alarm woke her at seven the next morning, it was to the realisation that she had completed none of the last-minute preparations she had planned to do on her last evening in England, and that once the taxi had deposited her home the day before she had managed to get up the stairs, into her flat and into bed, and that was all, such had been her exhaustion.

Consequently, the two hours before Hawk arrived were spent in a mad dash that left no room for apprehension or doubts, and when the doorbell rang, spot on nine o'clock, she was just ready.

'Hi.' He was lounging against the outer wall when she opened the door, big and dark in a long charcoal overcoat which was open over a grey business suit and pale blue shirt. His cool self-assurance was staggering.

'You haven't changed your mind, then?' He nodded to her suitcase, placed in readiness at the side of the door, as he spoke, and she forced an answering smile that nearly cracked her face.

'Hardly.'

'It's been done before.' The handsome face was cynical.

'Not by me,' she said carefully. 'If I agree to something I carry it through, difficult though you may find that to believe.'

'I don't find it difficult.' His eyes narrowed to blue slits as he spoke, the intensity of the piercing gaze unnerving, and she had the strange unaccountable impression he was on tenterhooks about something and endeavouring to conceal it—although what she couldn't begin to imagine.

He picked up the lightest of the three cases, tucking it under one arm before lifting the other two, which weighed a ton, with an ease that told her the powerful body was as finely honed as she had suspected.

'Any last-minute goodbyes?' he asked quietly as she joined him on the landing after closing the front door.

'No, just the key to pop through the letterbox of the flat below.' Now the moment had come she had none of the turmoil of the day before, merely a sense of inevitability. 'I said all my farewells yesterday.'

'Except one.' Dark eyebrows rose quizzically.

'Who?' She stared at him in surprise.

'Me,' he said softly.

'But I haven't left you,' she replied quickly. 'You're coming with me.'

'Ah, yes.' He smiled slowly and her skin began to tingle as the dark, alien side of him took over her senses. 'So our goodbyes are yet to be said?' It was said in a slightly amused voice but again the feeling that there was more below the surface had her staring at him with a straight face, her eyes big and golden in the cream of her skin and her hair framing her face like shimmering fire.

Once in the taxi he chatted easily about this and that, his manner relaxed and informal, but she had her work cut out to appear normal, the proximity of the big muscled body so close to hers sending little shock waves through every nerve and sinew with each tiny movement he made.

'Relax, Joanne.'

'What?' One moment he had been relating an amusing story about a business colleague they both knew, the next the hard blue gaze had fastened on her face and his hand had covered hers, his flesh warm and firm.

'You're nervous, on edge, and there's no need to be,' he said softly.

There's every need. 'I...I know that; I'm fine.'

'Little liar.' It was said quietly, his eyes skimming her face before coming to rest on her mouth, their touch like a warm caress. 'Is it just the unknown that puts that touch of fear in your eyes, Joanne?' he murmured. 'Or are you frightened of me too, of how it could be if you let it happen?'

'What?'

'Don't tell me you haven't felt it because I won't believe it; I've seen the reflection of what I feel in your eyes,' he said huskily. 'You wonder what it would feel like to be close to me, really close, for me to make love to you. You want me, Joanne; you can't deny it. You want me every bit as much as I want you.'

'You're mad.' She stared at him shakily, the fear of which he had spoken turning her eyes dark.

'No, merely honest. It's the most natural thing in the world for a man and woman to be attracted to each other; there's nothing wrong in it, and our physical chemistry is so hot it's sizzling.'

'You're talking about an affair.' She couldn't believe this conversation was taking place, but at the same time it was almost as though she had been waiting for just this from the first moment she had laid eyes on him.

'I'm talking about enjoyment, the giving and receiving of pleasure,' he said softly. 'I want you, Joanne, I admit it; I haven't felt like this in a long, long time. We could be good together; I could make you want me in a way you've never wanted a man before.'

'Hawk—'

'What was his name, Joanne, the man who made you retreat into this formidable glass tower you inhabit?' he asked with a sudden intensity. 'Whatever he meant to you, whatever it was like, with me it will be better. I would always be totally honest, there would be no guessing games, no cruelty. When it was over, whoever ended it, it would be quick and final—'

'I don't want a relationship with you.' He was propositioning her on the one hand and telling her he would finish it cleanly on the other? she thought dazedly, anger providing a welcome shot of adrenalin that went some way to quelling the hurt. How dared he? How *dared* he assume she was just waiting to fall into his arms like an overripe peach? And what about him anyway? If anyone retreated into towers it was him, although his were made of inches-thick steel.

'Yes, you do, although you can't bring yourself to admit it,' he said with an assuredness that hit her on the raw.

She stared at him icily, and something of her utter outrage must have got through because he took his hand from over hers, leaning back in his corner of the cab as he surveyed her with narrowed blue eyes.

'Does my taking the job in France have anything to do with this conversation?' she snapped tightly. 'And I want this wonderful truth that you're always going on about, mind.'

'I offered you the position at Bergique & Son because I feel you would be an asset to the Mallen Corporation,' Hawk said coolly. 'Any personal liaison with me is something quite separate.'

'But it wouldn't go amiss to have a nice warm bed waiting for you when you visit?' she asked tartly. And any emotional involvement would mean he was completely sure of her loyalty to the Mallen empire. That, probably, was what all this was about; he was certainly cold-blooded enough to think that way. Oh, he was just a cynical brute of a man. And to think she had actually been *grateful* for all his apparent thoughtfulness yesterday, for the way he had steered her through the last difficult goodbyes, for his generosity over the leaving party, for his accompanying her to France to ease the way for her. *Ease the way!* Fury combined with humiliation at her naivety. It had all been about trying to manipulate her to his will, and in such a way that Hawk, and the Mallen empire, couldn't lose.

'I take it that's a no to my suggestion we get to know each other better?' he asked drily.

'Dead right.' It was scathing.

'Pity. Patience is not normally one of my virtues but it looks as though I'll have to draw on hitherto unused resources,' he drawled slowly. 'But I can wait, Joanne, when I have to. And something tells me you are well worth waiting for.'

'Do you expect me to thank you for that observation?' she asked cuttingly, praying that the trembling in her stomach wouldn't reveal itself to the rapier-sharp gaze.

'It would be nice.'

The dark amusement was the last straw. 'Hawk, whatever impression I might have given you I don't go in for tawdry little affairs,' she said tightly, her voice quivering with the force of her emotion. 'When I give myself to a man it will be because I love him, all of him, not just his body or the cheap thrill of a few weeks or months of sexual gymnastics—'

'Wait there a moment.' He cut into her fury with a raised hand as he straightened in his seat. 'What are you saying here? You aren't asking me to believe that you haven't…' His voice trailed away and hot colour washed over her in a burning flood as it dawned on her what she had revealed. 'I don't believe it…'

'I'm not asking you to *believe* anything,' she said with

as much dignity as she could muster in the circumstances, 'and whatever interpretation you put on my words is your own; I have no intention of explaining anything to you.'

'Joanne—'

'I just value myself as something more than a body on two legs, all right?' Or as a useful little tool for the Mallen empire, she thought hotly as the humiliation and embarrassment became almost more than she could bear. Oh, why hadn't she kept *quiet*?

Hawk was used to shrewd businesswomen, or rich young females who flitted from one affair to another like graceful, bored butterflies, or—oh, a million and one other connotations on the theme. One thing he wasn't used to were twenty-nine-year-old virgins who acted like outraged paragons when he suggested they might get to know each other better—albeit very much better, she thought weakly.

Not that she was ashamed of what and who she was— she wasn't; she just hadn't meant to broadcast it to the one person, above all others, who would be sure to treat the news with contempt.

Not that Hawk Mallen looked contemptuous—stunned would have been a better description, she thought flatly. No doubt he was already regretting the waste of a couple of days when he could have been frying other, more obliging fish. The thought prompted her to say, but not with as much tartness as she would have liked, 'I think it better that I go to France alone in the circumstances.'

'What circumstances are you referring to? I wasn't aware anything had altered.' He met her eyes as he spoke, and Joanne wasn't to know it was the finest piece of bluffing Hawk Mallen had ever indulged in—and that in the dog-eat-dog world of high business where a poker face and an expressionless voice could mean the gain or loss of millions.

The flight to France, and journey to Bergique & Son which was situated in the heart of Paris, was conducted in a tense, screaming silence that had Joanne's nerves stretched as tightly as piano wire by the time they arrived at the pleasant, stone-clad building close to the Seine.

Hawk had said very little since their conversation in the taxi in England. Beyond pointing out one or two of the sights to her once they were in the car on the other side of the Channel he had only spoken to enquire if she was comfortable on the plane, if she would like a drink, and other such social niceties. Joanne had answered him in monosyllables, not because she was trying to be awkward but because she could only manage to force one or two words past the constriction in her throat.

It didn't help that the elegantly attractive stewardesses hadn't been able to keep their eyes off him either—she was sure that given the least bit of encouragement he would have had two telephone numbers pressed on him, and in spite of her earlier rejection of his advances it had rankled—painfully. He was a free agent, all the model-type beauties in the world could come on to him and she wouldn't have the slightest right to object, but…it still rankled.

She had found herself watching him from under her eyelashes, seeing how he responded to the subtle—and once or twice not so subtle—overtures by the two glamorous women, but he hadn't even appeared to notice them. Not that that meant anything, she told herself tetchily. With all the women who no doubt threw themselves at him every day of the week he could afford to be choosy. And that brought her back to the unescapable conclusion she had been forced to earlier, which was hurting more and more despite her telling herself, every minute, every second, that she was a complete and utter fool to care.

Hawk Mallen had a whole host of adoring females

who would be only too pleased to be at his beck and call; he needed another one like a hole in the head. So why had he propositioned her? Partly because he was attracted to her, yes, she had to give him that, but also because it would be very useful for him to have a nice devoted mistress installed at Bergique & Son to keep an eye on things for him, and also oblige with a warm bed when he deigned to visit France. Two birds with one stone. Clever.

'Bergique & Son. We've arrived.' They had just drawn up outside the three-storeyed, endlessly long structure, set in one of the great boulevards that had Paris's unmistakable stamp about it, and as Joanne gazed through the car window she felt a little shiver slither down her spine.

This apparently innocuous building was where she was going to prove herself over the next few months, or fail miserably, and after all that had happened earlier that day it was suddenly a matter of life or death that it was the former prospect.

She had to prove she wasn't a naive, ingenuous type of individual, but an intelligent career woman who was as much in charge of her private life as her career, that she knew exactly where she was going and how to get there. Because Hawk Mallen would be looking on, for sure, albeit from a distance, assessing, judging, probing. He was...formidable.

'Joanne?' Her head shot round to meet his; there had been that certain note in his voice she had heard just a few times before—soft, caressing. 'I want you to succeed here; I'm not your enemy.'

'I...I know.' She tried to sound convincing.

'No, I don't think you do.' His blue eyes had turned to glittering silver in the sunlight streaming through the car window and his mouth was rueful, sensuous, turning her limbs liquid and sending the blood racing through her veins. 'I want you, I have no intention of pretending otherwise, but that doesn't mean I'll behave like a sulky little boy if you don't want to share the warmth of my bed. You can rely on my backing, one hundred per cent, for anything you see fit to do within Bergique & Son.'

'Thank you,' she murmured quietly. She didn't know what to think; did anyone know what to think around Hawk Mallen? 'You must see it's better we keep our relationship on a business footing?'

'Must I?' He was watching her intently, his narrowed eyes roaming over her flushed face as her gaze fell from his. 'Why?'

'Because it wouldn't work; I'm different to you,' she said firmly.

'It's the difference that has me up at two in the morning having cold showers,' he said huskily.

The confession was unexpected and as her gaze met his again she saw raw hunger in the dark male face.

'Hawk, I'm going to be based in France, and you…you're all round the world. You just want an affair, some fun when you visit—'

'No, you are wrong; I want more than that,' he said softly. 'You have got into my head, my bones, my blood; I have never trodden so carefully with a woman before, Joanne.' She stared at him, knowing that the punchline was going to follow, and it did.

'But I have to be honest too,' he said with a curious flatness. 'Women always complicate things by talking about love, when what they really mean is passion, desire, and I have learnt it is kinder from the outset to lay down the rules of play.'

He meant it; he really thought he was being fair, ethical in his cold-bloodedness, she thought faintly. She paused a moment, and then took a deep breath before she said, 'You don't believe two people can fall in love and live happily ever after?'

The driver of the firm's car, a long black limousine with lusciously soft leather upholstery, had been waiting outside to open Hawk's door for the last few moments, and now Hawk wound down his window and told him to carry the cases into the building, before rewinding it and turning to Joanne.

'I don't believe in happy ever after, no,' he said quietly, the devastatingly attractive face deadly serious. 'Look at the statistics, for crying out loud. I can believe in the power of obsession, sexual or otherwise, and I know desire and passion are real, but the notion of two people promising to stay together for the rest of their lives is pure folly, Joanne. Men and women can have good strong relationships, but inevitably that first sexual thrill dies and then, if they are locked into a marriage contract, one or the other of them will cause misery by sleeping with someone else.'

He stared at her unflinchingly, his sapphire gaze hard. 'The best relationships are the ones unclouded by any messy emotion,' he said evenly, 'where both partners have their eyes wide open.'

The basic idea behind Hawk's words—that love was an elusive dream without real form or credibility—was so near everything she had told herself in her youth and miserable teenage years that for a moment the past was more real than the present, and she felt the shock of it jolt her heart violently; but then an inner voice made itself heard.

She might have been sceptical, wary of love and the promises that went with it, but that time was past. Something had happened and she knew what she believed now—that there was something finer, more noble, more lasting than mere sexual involvement and an agreement of minds, or cold-blooded business arrangements where men and women slept together to further their careers.

Something of what she was feeling must have shown in her face because Hawk turned to look straight ahead, and now his profile was cold. 'It's dangerous to let yourself be fooled, Joanne,' he said flatly.

'I can't agree—'

'When my parents died so unexpectedly I had to go through their papers, personal and otherwise,' he said levelly, interrupting her as though she hadn't spoken. 'I found my mother's diaries...' There was a pause and then he said, 'They were a catalogue of despair and heartache and bitter grief. It would seem my father had had affairs from their fourth or fifth year of marriage, and they had broken my mother's heart, destroyed her self-esteem and turned her into someone she clearly didn't like.'

She didn't dare make any sound or movement; besides, she wouldn't have known what to say.

'The diaries acknowledged he still cared for her in his own way, as a friend, companion, but she wasn't enough for him; that was the truth of the matter however he tried to explain the other women away. My grandfather knew what was happening; in fact it had caused a final wedge between him and my father that was insurmountable and was a further complication between my parents.'

'But your grandfather didn't agree because he had loved his own wife so much,' Joanne said gently. 'Surely that must tell you that love is a real emotion?'

'They only had two years together before she died,' Hawk said quietly. 'Who knows what would have happened if my grandmother had lived?'

'Do you believe that—*really* believe it?' she asked huskily.

He turned his head and met the honey-brown gaze, and for a long moment, as he looked into the velvet orbs, he said nothing.

'Do you?' she persisted.

There was a flicker in the silver-blue eyes, a veiling of his thoughts, and then he said, 'Yes, I do. But I have been very remiss—this is neither the time nor the place for such a conversation, and you must be anxious to meet everyone now you are here.'

'It's all right—'

'No, it isn't. Forgive me.' He had retreated again, and so completely it was like a slap in the face.

The next two hours sped by in a whirl of introductions, numerous offices, social pleasantries and different faces, and over it all, every minute, every second, Joanne was aware of Hawk's dark, brooding presence on the perimeter of her gaze.

There was a subdued furore everywhere they went— less to do with her appearance than with Hawk's, Joanne reflected wryly—and plenty of sycophantic chit-chat that indicated everyone was well aware of the precarious state of the firm and why new blood had been brought in. Pierre was conspicuous by his absence and his sylph-like secretary, Antoinette, a slender, graceful nineteen-year-old who stared at Joanne with great dark eyes and a carefully blank face, made his apologies in a neutral voice that gave nothing away.

Nevertheless, Joanne was aware the French girl didn't like her, and the knowledge was a little disconcerting, considering they would be working closely together in the future.

She would perhaps have been a little more concerned about Antoinette, the somewhat slipshod air of the firm in general, and her growing certainty that the job was going to be even harder than she had expected, if a large segment of her mind hadn't been taken up with Hawk's amazing revelation about his parents. His father's betrayal and his mother's anguish had affected him deeply, that much was obvious, but she couldn't rid herself of the impression that there was something more he hadn't told her, another complication that had driven the deep lines of cynicism into the sides of that sensuous mouth.

But he wouldn't tell her if there was. She glanced across at him now as he stood talking to Antoinette on the other side of the room, the beautiful French girl clearly hanging on his every word. Intuition told her he regretted revealing as much as he had already, and he wouldn't thank her for the impulse which had prompted it. He was a loner, the original wolf who walked alone, and to get mixed up with a man like him would be emotional suicide, even if she didn't love him.

Love him? The shock of the thought caused her to stare glassy-eyed at the young man who was trying to engage her in conversation, and she must have gone white because he immediately suggested she sit down, that he fetch her a glass of water, or perhaps she needed some fresh air? 'It has been a long day for you.' The French voice with its sexy accent was ingratiatingly concerned. 'Yes?'

'Yes.' She aimed for a lightness she was far from feeling. 'But productive.' Act normally, put this to the back of your mind till later, talk, *smile*...

It was another half an hour before Hawk suggested he take her to the apartment which had been rented for her as part of the job package, and every single muscle in her face and body was so tense she felt like one giant ache. She couldn't risk the luxury of thinking; she was working on automatic and dealing purely with the absolute present—what she could see and hear and feel. If she started to think she would become petrified, or burst into tears, or shout and scream, and none of the options were attractive.

'You handled that just fine.' The American drawl was more obvious than normal as they walked out of the building and over to the car which had just been brought round to the front. 'I'm impressed.'

'Are they, though?' She smiled as she said it but he caught the underlying tension that made her voice over-bright.

'I think so.' He opened the car door for her and the piercing blue gaze watched her as she slid into the back of the car. 'And if they're not they soon will be.' He was leaning on the top of the door as he spoke and for a moment their eyes caught and held before he straightened, shutting the door with a soft slam.

Why did he have to do that—be so…nice? she asked herself savagely as he walked round the back of the car and slid into the seat beside her, tapping the glass divide once he was seated and indicating for the driver to pull away. Solicitude and tact didn't come naturally with Hawk Mallen—she had observed him in action for weeks and a barracuda couldn't be more ruthless—and it made the gentleness he had just displayed terribly seductive.

The late afternoon sky had darkened in the last hour, black storm clouds looming threateningly in the October twilight, but Joanne could see the slender spire of the Notre Dame, the Grande Dame of Paris, against the grey sky as the first drops of rain began to splatter against the car windows.

'We're in for a storm.' Hawk glanced at her, his male bulk big and alien in the car's interior. 'I was going to suggest we tour round for a while, see some of the sights and have a meal, but perhaps you'd rather go straight to the apartment?'

'Yes, please.' In spite of the spaciousness within the limousine his nearness was making her breathless.

'Your alacrity is a little dampening,' he said drily, his sapphire eyes glittering in the darkness of his face. 'Is my company really so hard to take?'

'I didn't mean it like that,' she protested weakly.

'No?' He smiled, that wonderfully elusive sexy smile that he used so rarely but with such devastating effect. 'Then I might get a cup of coffee in your new home?'

'But what about him?' She gestured agitatedly at the driver.

'Three's a crowd if that's what you mean, but don't worry, I have no intention of making the poor guy hang about waiting for me,' Hawk said easily. 'I'll get a cab from your place to my hotel, okay?'

Her place. She stared at him, her brain refusing to function. 'But…' He wasn't going to take no for an answer; she could see it in the sudden narrowing of his eyes. 'I haven't anything in; I haven't even *seen* the apartment yet—'

'No problem.' His gaze traced the outline of her lips, making her flesh tingle. 'I had the concierge take care of that.'

'Oh.' That was that, then; Hawk Mallen had spoken and the rest of the world could only obey—

'I know I should wait until I am asked, but I have the nasty feeling I would wait a long time, Joanne.' His voice was suspiciously humble now as though he had read her thoughts—which he had—but in spite of the knowledge she was being duped she just couldn't resist the little-boy charm.

'Well, if you've the time…' she said helplessly, the anger that had risen at his arrogance magically gone.

'That I have.' He grinned suddenly, his eyes wicked. 'The pleasure of a few minutes in your company is worth any sacrifice—'

'Oh, *please*…' Her voice was sarcastic but she couldn't help smiling back, even as the warning bells began to ring loud and hard. He was dangerous, so, so dangerous, and never more than now, when he was wielding that powerful magnetism for his own purposes, his eyes merciless as they took in her flushed confusion. She ought to tell him she was tired, that it had been one hell of a day, that she needed time alone to sort out the muddle of her thoughts, all of which would be true.

But she wasn't going to—her eyes darkened at her stupidity—because she wanted to be with him for a few minutes more. She wanted to have him to herself, to know that he was concentrating on her and her alone. He didn't love her, she knew that, but she had spelt out the rules of play loud and clear that morning, and if he still wanted to spend time in her company, knowing how she felt, surely that was all right? She was trying to justify herself against the accusing voice in her head telling her she was playing with fire, even as she acknowledged she had no defence.

Hawk slid aside the glass partition separating them from the driver, giving the address of her apartment before explaining their change of plan and then settling back comfortably in his seat.

She was vaguely aware of the street cafés, elegant architecture and unmistakable ambience which was Paris as the car bowled along wide boulevards, but the excitement, the magic, was all enclosed within the car for Joanne.

It was utter madness, the worst sort of foolishness, to fall for a man like Hawk Mallen, she acknowledged desperately, her heart thudding a tattoo as the electricity within the car became frightening; but if he didn't *know*, surely she was safe? He thought she was merely attracted to him on a physical level, he'd made that plain, so all she had to do was maintain the principles she'd set that morning. Simple really...

The apartment was situated in the north of Paris, in Montmartre, which seemed to Joanne very much a little village in its own right. Although the bustling centre was a hive of activity, the area in the north-east where her modern apartment block stood, shaded by large trees, was more quiet, with an abundance of green parkland and sleepy museums.

'I thought you would prefer something restful to come home to after a hard day's work,' Hawk said quietly as the driver unloaded her luggage and Hawk's overnight bag from the limousine, 'and La Villette is one of the gentler spots in Paris.'

'It's lovely.' Joanne managed a smile as Hawk sent the driver on his way and picked up all the luggage, a bag under each arm and suitcases in either hand, before leading the way through the paved garden with fountain and up the five broad steps to the front door.

The concierge was there immediately they stepped into the elegant foyer, a small dapper man who was all smiles and teeth. 'Monsieur Mallen, Mademoiselle Crawford, welcome, welcome.' The high, excited voice matched his appearance, and he barely paused for breath before saying, 'Everything is ready as you requested, Monsieur Mallen; I am sure Mademoiselle Crawford will be most comfortable, but if there is anything I can do, anything at all…'

'Merci.' Hawk was polite but firm. 'I'm sure Mademoiselle Crawford will call if she needs you, Gérard. There is no need to accompany us; I have the key.'

'But the cases, Monsieur—'

'No problem.' Hawk cut short the anguished protest by the simple expedient of pushing a folded note in the little man's hand before striding purposefully to the lift, Joanne following in his wake.

'Merci, Monsieur Mallen, merci beaucoup.'

It had clearly been a generous tip, Joanne reflected wryly as the concierge continued to beam rapturously while Hawk placed their luggage in the lift and drew Joanne in beside him, the little man only turning to prance away as the lift doors began to close. And then a sudden thought struck her. 'You seem to know your way around,' she said suspiciously. 'Have you been here before?'

'Of course.' The vivid blue eyes with their thick black lashes looked straight at her as he said, 'You didn't think I would take an apartment for you without checking it out first?'

'You?' She realised her mouth was open and shut it with a little snap.

'Yes, me.' He smiled lazily. 'I had Antoinette do the donkey work and narrow it down to three suitable places from which I chose this one.'

'I see.' And she did. This, then, was to be his love-nest in France, and no doubt there were others in different parts of the world, perhaps with other 'manager-esses' keeping them warm? 'Why?'

'Because it was the most suitable.' He knew that wasn't what she had meant—she could tell so from the sardonic gleam in his eyes—but short of asking him outright if he had an ulterior motive in looking over her new home she couldn't say much more. But she didn't like this; she didn't like it at all, she thought silently.

'Gérard lives on the ground floor just off the foyer,' Hawk continued evenly, 'and nothing much gets past him. I like that.' The lift slid to a halt and he bent to pick up the cases again as he added, 'You can't be too careful in this day and age.'

Indeed you can't, she thought tightly as she glanced at the black head, the short, springy hair shining with virile health. But her concern was less in the nature of a possible intruder than the man a foot or so away from her, who had turned her life upside down and inside out over the last few weeks.

'Stop frowning and come and see your new abode.'

She opened her mouth to say she wasn't frowning as

he straightened, but then realised she was and hastily smoothed her features as the piercing gaze came her way again.

They stepped from the lift into ankle-deep carpeting, and as Hawk moved across the small cream-coloured square of space to the front door, setting down the cases and inserting a key in the lock, she stared about her bewilderedly. 'Where are all the other apartments?'

'There is one on each floor, five in all,' Hawk said easily. 'This is the top one to give you more of a view.'

'Hawk—'

But he had already stepped into the apartment and she had no choice but to follow him in. It was the last word in luxury, and immediately the concierge's fawning behaviour became clear. This wasn't the sort of place normal people, like her, lived in, she thought helplessly. This was way out of her league, job or no job. She could never afford this—

'Do you like it?' He was watching her face very carefully although in her shock she wasn't aware of it.

'Like it?' The room they had entered was an elegant drawing room in pale blue and yellow which seemed to stretch endlessly—impressive, beautiful, with dark wood furniture and a beautiful suite, TV, hi-fi, bar... 'I can't afford this, Hawk, you know that,' she said tightly, anger curling through her stomach.

'It's part of the package,' he said expressionlessly. 'I thought you realised that.'

Keep calm; match him for coolness. Her brain was giving orders she obeyed automatically. 'This is not a normal apartment,' she said evenly, 'and you know it.'

'Normality is relative.' He walked across the room to the fireplace where a living-flame fire was flickering red and gold. 'I had this put in to make it more homely,' he said coolly.

'Hawk, this is ridiculous—'

'Come and see the view,' he interrupted authoritatively.

She joined him at the huge patio windows which opened on to a large balcony, beyond which it seemed as though all Paris was stretched out before her, taking great steadying breaths as she did so.

'Do you want to go outside?' he asked quietly.

'No, I do not.' It was clipped and terse.

'Come and see the rest of it, then,' he said calmly.

He wasn't giving her time to think, let alone talk; that much registered. He was bulldozing her along as though this were all *fait accompli*, and it wasn't. She couldn't *let* it be. What would people say? What obvious conclusion would they come to if she allowed him to install her in a place like this?

The rest of the apartment was equally superb—the separate dining room in pale gold, the massive fitted kitchen and breakfast area, the *en suite* bathroom, a splendid marbled construction in cream and honeybrown, and the bedroom with its huge four-poster bed and silk hangings. It was all incredible, larger than life— very much like Hawk Mallen, Joanne thought as the anger began to take over, flushing her cheeks scarlet.

'You must see I can't live here, Hawk.' She faced him after the tour in the same spot they had started in, just inside the front door. 'It would make my position at Bergique & Son impossible from the start.'

'Why?' The huge, high-ceilinged room suited him perfectly; he had perfect domination over his surroundings as he stood watching her silently, his hands thrust in his pockets and his blue eyes narrowed like lasers on her hot face.

'You don't need to ask that, surely, not a man of the world like you?' she said cuttingly. 'Everyone would assume I was your mistress; you know they would.'

'I would have thought that could only strengthen your

position,' he said with outrageous arrogance. 'Give you
the sort of edge you need.'

'I don't need an edge from you.' She drew herself up
straight, her face fiery. 'I'll sink or swim by my own
efforts, thank you—'

'Don't be so childish.' The complete lack of emotion
in his voice and face made her even madder.

'Childish?' Her voice was far too shrill but she didn't
care. 'I'm not so childish that I don't know why you've
rented this place, Hawk Mallen. And that little man
downstairs knew too, didn't he? In fact the whole world
and his wife probably know.'

'Perhaps you'd like to be more specific?' he said
softly.

'Do I have to spell it out?' she hissed furiously, his
composure all the more irritating when she was so up-
tight she could barely speak.

'Humour me.' There was a thread of steel in the gravelly voice now but for once it didn't intimidate her.
Whatever he said, however he explained it away, she
just *knew* he had originally set this place up thinking she
would become his mistress. How dared he? *How dare
he* assume so much?!

'You thought I would allow myself to be bought,
didn't you?' she accused grimly, watching him with angry eyes as he crossed the room to stand just in front of
her, his big body formidable. 'You arranged all this, the
apartment, everything, thinking I would agree to sleep
with you. I know it's the truth, Hawk, whether you admit
it or not.'

'I wouldn't insult your intelligence by pretending anything else.'

It was said coolly, and without the slightest shred of
embarrassment, and for a moment she was so taken
aback she just stared at him before her hand lashed out

and connected with the tanned skin of his face in a ringing slap.

'You...you—'

'Now just hold on there.' He caught one hand, and
then the other, as she attempted to hit him again, and
she saw, with a measure of satisfaction despite the circumstances, that his cool had quite gone. 'Hold on a
damn minute, will you, woman? I admit I'd hoped we
might get together when I looked at this place, but that
wasn't the sole reason for buying it. I wanted to know
you were safe, in a good environment and with some
protection—'

'You liar—'

'I never lie, Joanne,' he said grimly. 'If you had
agreed to start a relationship with me that would have
been the icing on the cake, of course it would, I admit
it, damn it, but there was never any question of *buying*
you. I know enough about you to realise you can't be
bought.'

'Do you? Do you indeed?' she shot back furiously.
'Then tell me, if the new manager were old and ugly,
or married, would you have got this particular apartment? Is this the normal sort of package you give to new
employees you aren't worried about impressing?'

He stared at her for a good thirty seconds, his face
working, and she knew he wanted to deny it but also
that he couldn't, the devastating honesty that was an
integral part of him blocking the words, and then he
pulled her against him, so violently she almost lost her
breath before his mouth swooped down on hers in a kiss
that was all fire and fury.

'No!'

She fought him—afterwards she reminded herself
over and over that she had fought him—but it had been
too late the moment his lips had touched hers. That very
second she had begun to drown in a multitude of sen-

sations that had no rhyme or reason to them, her love for him taking over so completely that what was all wrong felt terrifyingly right.

He had moulded her into his frame from that first moment, his male body encompassing hers in a manner as old as time, the perfect jigsaw, and she was left in no doubt as to the state of his arousal.

And he knew. He *knew* her resistance was paper-thin, because after the first few minutes his hold on her slackened, just enough to prove she was in his arms because she wanted to be.

She moaned, she couldn't help it, as he began to nip and taste and savour her mouth, exciting her so seductively, so expertly that she was quivering and moist in his arms when the kiss was no longer light and teasing, but a declaration of intent.

Joanne shivered helplessly as the sensuous mouth played with her shell-like ears before moving to the sensitive skin of her throat, seeking the slight swell of her cleavage just visible under her businesslike blouse. He was good, he was so, so good, and although she knew he didn't feel the same, that he had stated exactly what she could expect from him, her heightened emotions were quelling all lucid thought.

There was electricity flowing through her veins instead of blood; she could feel it in every nerve and sinew as it created an ache that was unbearable.

His body heat released the faint trace of expensive aftershave that was still on his skin, and she couldn't believe what the erotic fragrance did to her senses, entwined as she was in his arms.

He thrust his tongue into her mouth, in the same way he wanted to thrust into the warm, pliable female body that was so soft and fluid against his strong male frame, and as he felt her answering response sensation exploded through him like raw fire, causing him to become rock-hard.

'Joanne, Joanne...' His breathing was ragged as the palms of his hands slid over the smooth silky skin of her stomach, the warmth of her, the slight moisture on her flesh, creating a pleasure-pain that was overwhelming.

All that had happened earlier that day—the knowledge that he was manipulating her, the whole situation, to his and the Mallen Corporation's advantage—just didn't seem to bear any weight when she was in his arms. Joanne knew it—a tiny rational part of her mind was shouting the warning with all its might—but it was in-effective against the bewilderingly new sensations she was experiencing for the first time.

His hands were in the glowing red silk of her hair, pulling her head gently back to tilt her mouth for greater invasion.

Was this how her mother had felt with the man who had given her her one and only child? Joanne asked her-self helplessly. She had always sensed her mother had felt something special for her father—not that she had ever admitted it, but despite her bitterness and resent-ment that Joanne looked like him there had always been a longing in her eyes when she had spoken his name that hadn't been there with all the others.

Perhaps she *had* felt like this; perhaps you only felt like this once in a lifetime and that was why her mother had wasted the rest of her life trying to find that elusive feeling again?

Her body was boneless now, her legs trembling so much it was only Hawk's arms holding her against him which were keeping her upright, and she could hear her-self murmuring his name, *moaning* his name, as he rav-ished her throat in an agony of desire.

And then, shockingly, unbelievably, just when she thought he was going to draw her down on to the thick

deep carpet and she would have to find some strength
to fight him, if she could, he moved her out of his arms
and walked to the door.

His voice told her—its deep tones penetrating the fog
of desire that still held her in its seductive grip—that she
should get a good night's sleep, that she was tired, and,
lastly, that he would see her in the morning.

CHAPTER SIX

TWICE. It had happened twice, and she was going to make darn sure there wouldn't be a third time.

Joanne had sunk down on to the carpet as Hawk had left, her shaking legs unable to hold her a moment longer, and had remained there for long minutes with tears streaming down her face. How could she have been so weak as to let him walk all over her like that? she'd asked herself over and over again through the tearing pain, before forcing herself to rise and walk slowly into the bathroom, where she had washed her tear-stained face with trembling hands.

She stared at herself now in the mirror, her eyes still liquid with the tears she was holding back by sheer will-power and her nose red and shiny.

What had it all been? An exercise in subjecting her to his will? A demonstration of his power and authority? The cruellest sort of proof that he could take or leave her despite all her brave words? Probably a mixture of all of those things, she thought bleakly, brushing a strand of damp hair off her face and shutting her eyes tight for a moment. If he had continued the lovemaking she would have found it difficult to resist full intimacy, and she would have hated herself afterwards, and him too. But she would still have loved him and that was more scary.

So... She opened her eyes and narrowed her gaze on the blotchy face in the mirror. Pull yourself together, girl. Nothing has happened, not really, even if it was more by luck than judgement. She wasn't sure why he hadn't followed through on his advantage; probably he thought he was softening her up for the kill? Or maybe once she was in his arms her inexperience had turned him off? Or perhaps—

'Stop it, stop it, stop it.' She spoke the words out loud through clenched teeth, as angry with herself as she was with him. The whys and wherefores didn't matter, not really. Whatever his motives she was taking this as a warning that one little moth had got terribly near the flames that could easily consume it, and it wasn't going to happen again. She shook her head savagely. No way.

'What the hell are you talking about?' Hawk asked tightly.

'I'm moving out this morning; I mean it.'

'*Joanne.*'

'You can "Joanne" me all you like, Hawk, but I *mean* it.' He had just arrived at the apartment to inform her the firm's car was waiting downstairs, his eyes immediately narrowing on her suitcases and bag near the front door, but she had faced him bravely in spite of the fact that her insides were melted jelly. She couldn't remember ever feeling such humiliation and embarrassment before, but she would rather die than let him know, she thought grimly, staring resolutely into his angry face.

'Joanne, I haven't the time or the patience for this,' he said coldly.

'Tough.' It wasn't quite the way to talk to one's employer, she thought with a touch of hysteria, but then Hawk Mallen wasn't the average boss. 'I'm bringing my bags with me and I'll move into a hotel until I find something within my price range; we can sort out a reasonable allowance for accommodation later.'

'I don't believe this is happening.'

He didn't look as though he did either, she thought weakly, and he had never looked more gorgeous, which she really didn't need.

'You are seriously telling me you won't stay here?' he said, after a good thirty seconds when they had stared at each other like two gladiators in mortal combat. His voice held a touch of bemused incredulity and it made her want to laugh—something she had thought last night would never happen again. 'The place has a lease for six months.'

'That's not my problem.' She could see he was freshly shaved, the tanned skin begging to be touched— She cut the thought firmly and returned to the attack. 'I am not prepared to be talked about, Hawk, and neither do I want to stay on here under false pretences. You clearly had something other than a work relationship in mind when you took this apartment, and as I have no intention of fulfilling that requirement—' if he mentioned last night she would kill him, on the spot '—I wouldn't be comfortable continuing here.'

'You really *are* serious.' How could someone so soft and small and kitten-like be so *unreasonable*? Hawk asked himself furiously. 'Joanne, this is crazy.'

'I don't think so; it would be crazy to stay here, though.' She could see she had totally thrown him and it felt so good, so wonderfully good, after the miserable night she'd had when she'd walked the beautiful apartment till dawn. She wanted to hate him, all through the long dark night hours she had tried to hate him, but although her head was in agreement her heart just wouldn't fall into line. He was the epitome of the love-'em-and-leave-'em types her mother had fallen for, she'd told herself angrily—only after one thing, shallow, heartless—but still, as the first pink rays had crept over the balcony floor, her heart had wept for what might have been.

'That's your last word on the matter?' he asked grimly.

'Yes.' She stared at him a little nervously now, wondering what he was going to do.

'Right.' He walked across to the telephone and picked it up, tapping in the number in a manner that could only be termed vicious. 'Antoinette?' His voice was icy. 'Miss Crawford and myself won't be in the office till this afternoon, and cancel the lease on Miss Crawford's apartment, would you? It isn't suitable.'

The French girl must have been as surprised as Hawk had been, because he next said, the words bitten out through clenched teeth, 'For a number of reasons,' and then, 'I don't care about that; pay the damn thing in full,' before slamming down the receiver so hard it jumped up again.

'Right, we flat-hunt.' He glared at her, his eyes blue ice. 'Satisfied?'

'You don't have to do that; I can find something later and stay in a hotel for now—'

'I am not leaving France until I see you settled in suitable accommodation that I have personally inspected, right?' The glare intensified. 'You don't know Paris, the safe and not so safe areas, and frankly you are a conman's dream.'

'I am not!' she protested hotly, her cheeks burning scarlet.

'Yes, you are,' he countered, his voice deep now, too deep, its texture making shivers dance down her spine as he eyed her grimly. 'How you've got to the age of twenty-nine without being snared by some man a little bolder than the rest I don't know,' he said darkly. 'Perhaps it's because you're just too good to be true.'

She didn't know if he was being nasty now, especially in view of her abandonment last night, but she couldn't think of anything to say anyway, just staring at him with big, wary honey-brown eyes as she forced herself not to wilt.

'Come on.' He turned to the door, his voice suddenly brisk. 'I had planned to leave France this afternoon; my work schedule is hellish and I haven't got time to waste. I know the agents Antoinette used to find this place; we'll give them a visit.'

'I don't want anything like this—'

'Trust me.' It was said tongue-in-cheek but his eyes weren't angry now, and she had to fight against the flood of relief and joy filling her body. He wanted to find her somewhere where she would be safe; he cared enough for that? Don't be stupid! The voice in her head answered the spurt of hope immediately. You're here to do a job for him and he wants you one hundred per cent the capable machine he expects. If there were difficulties it would affect your work; that is all he is thinking of.

Hawk didn't leave France that afternoon. It was four o'clock before they found her an apartment, after visiting several others scattered all over the city, but immediately she saw it she knew it was the one.

She had insisted on speaking to the agents herself, Hawk's idea of price range being in the super league, and had liked the sound of the converted house, three storeys high with the apartment occupying the top floor, in a quiet square close to the Latin Quarter.

The rain and wind of the night before had given way to weak sunshine when they reached the old cobbled square dotted with gnarled trees, benches complete with old men in berets and young grandchildren about their knees, and a general air of bygone tranquillity that sat well on the stately houses trying to maintain a semblance of dignity despite crumbling balconies and flaking paint. Joanne thought it was charming.

'Right, I've seen enough; on to the next one,' Hawk said abruptly as their long-suffering driver parked on the road opposite, and Hawk's gaze followed hers across to the sleepy square.

'Hang on a minute; I haven't seen the apartment yet,' Joanne protested quickly.

'You don't need to, surely?' Hawk said disparagingly.

'Of course I do.' She turned to him, a ray of autumn sunshine turning her smooth bob to red fire. 'It looks lovely.'

'Lovely?' The bemused incredulity was back. '*Lovely?* What, exactly, are you looking at, Joanne?'

'I'm looking at happy children with people who love them, who have got time to *care*, at a quiet little haven in the midst of all the busyness, at those wonderful old cobbles and ancient trees, at—' She stopped suddenly. 'Why? What are you looking at?'

The blue eyes stared back at her, moving over her creamy skin, fine eyebrows, small straight nose and generously full mouth, before returning to capture her gaze again.

'Hawk?' She knew she was blushing at the quiet scrutiny but she couldn't help it. 'What did you see?'

He turned his eyes to the square again, and this time his voice was without expression as he said, 'I saw old trees, a square that needs cleaning up and terraced houses that look like a good wind would blow them down.'

'That's what you see?' She shook her head slowly, the movement causing her hair to shimmer like liquid silk. 'Then I'm sorry for you, Hawk.'

'Don't be.' The reserve was back, stronger than ever, and his voice was frosty as he said, 'You intend to inspect this one, I gather?'

'Yes, I do.' He didn't like it but she couldn't help that, she thought silently.

'And you'll take it whatever now, yes?' he suggested grimly.

'You mean to spite you?'

'Exactly.'

'Is that what you think of me?' She was angry and she was glad of it; it helped to keep the hurt at bay. 'Then you won't want to come and see yourself, will you?' she challenged stiffly.

He didn't answer, giving her a long level look that was quite unreadable, before opening his door and walking round to hers and helping her alight, still without saying a word.

The plump, motherly landlady whose house it was occupied the ground floor, and, she told Joanne in French, the young couple who occupied the second floor were very friendly and very happy. 'Just married, you know?' she added with a beaming smile, her eyes narrowing slightly on Hawk.

'How nice.' Joanne managed a fairly normal smile but made sure within the next few moments that she made her working relationship to Hawk quite clear—there had been a definite matchmaking gleam in the Frenchwoman's eyes.

She didn't know exactly what to expect as she climbed the polished wood stairs—no executive lift here, she thought wryly—but when she reached the top floor and opened the door to the flat her first impression was the enormous capacity for light within the sitting room that faced her. The walls were painted cream, and a honey-fawn carpet and curtains emphasised the rays of mild golden sunshine streaming through the two floor-to-ceiling windows. There was no door to divide the sitting room from the kitchen and dining area, but the clever arrangement of the furniture made each section feel remarkably self-contained.

The pale colour scheme was carried through into the small bedroom and tiny bathroom, and although the square footage of the apartment was small—in fact the whole would probably have fitted with room to spare into the drawing room of the grand apartment she had left that morning—the general effect was one of space and light.

'I love it.' Joanne walked across to the minute balcony which led off one of the French windows, and was only large enough to accommodate two cane chairs and a small eighteen-inch table, and looked at the view across the square. 'And I'm not saying that to be awkward, incidentally,' she added, 'whatever you think.'

'It's small,' Hawk stated flatly.

'It's compact,' she countered quickly.

'And the area isn't the best you could do.'

'Hawk, I never have lived in the "best" areas,' Joanne said tightly, memories of the children's home, where she had spent the last few years of her childhood after her mother's second marriage had ended so disastrously, burning vividly on the screen of her mind. 'And, as you said yesterday, everything is relative.'

'That's not quite what I said.' He eyed her grimly for a moment, Madame Lemoine hovering in the doorway behind them. 'You're quite sure you won't reconsider the apartment in Montmartre?'

'Quite sure,' she stated firmly.

'And if we look at further apartments you'll come back to this one, won't you?' It was said with such an air of resignation that she wanted to smile, despite the bittersweet pain being with him induced.

She nodded slowly. 'It's friendly, Hawk, and...me somehow. I like it.'

'So be it.' He shot her one exasperated look before walking past and conferring with the little Frenchwoman, Joanne in the meantime wandering round inspecting cupboards and drawer space.

'You can move in tonight.' He came up behind her as she stood looking down into the square again to where an old man and two small children were feeding a noisy squad of jostling birds. 'If you want to, that is.' Madame Lemoine had bustled happily away.

'Yes, I do...thank you,' she murmured awkwardly. 'I...I'm sorry I've delayed you—'

She turned as she spoke, and when her eyes met his felt that little jolt of electricity she always experienced when the full power of the piercing blue gaze took hers.

'My choice.' The words were brief, concise; he was a man who rarely elaborated on the essential, which made it all the more remarkable when he added, 'The sunshine is turning your hair to living flame, do you know that? And your eyes are as dark as a night sky, although sometimes they're the shade of warm honey. Who do you get your colouring from—your mother or your father?' he asked softly.

The question hit her in the solar plexus but she didn't duck it. 'My mother was a natural blonde,' she said stiffly, 'but my father had red hair and brown eyes, according to her. She...she didn't like it, that I took after him.'

'One of the reasons for the foster homes?' he asked quietly.

He hadn't referred to their conversation on that first evening over the last few weeks, and she had convinced herself he had forgotten it, dismissed it as unimportant, although she realised now that was silly. Hawk Mallen forgot nothing about anyone—it was all noted and filed away in that computer-type brain in case it was useful for the future.

'Possibly.' She shrugged, lowering her head and aiming to sidle past him but he caught her shoulders in his large hands and held her fast.

'Was it rough?' he murmured gently. 'Your childhood? Is that why you hold the world in such distrust?'

'I don't.' The suggestion shocked her.

'Joanne, when someone who looks like you do has never formed a close relationship, there's something badly wrong.' His voice was steady and firm and it was clear he wasn't going to let go of either her or the conversation.

'I could say the same about you,' she shot back quickly.

'Yes, you could, but it wouldn't be true,' he said softly, and for a moment the import of his words didn't hit her. Then, as her eyes widened with the knowledge of what he had just admitted, and the pain and searing jealousy attacked in the same instant, he continued, 'But it was a long, long time ago, and anyway, we aren't discussing me.'

'We aren't discussing me either,' she snapped testily, wrenching herself out of his grasp. 'I work for you, Hawk, that's all, and my life is my own, past and present.'

'When do you have fun, Joanne?' He ignored her former words as though she hadn't spoken and it was terribly irritating. 'Or is that a three-letter word that doesn't feature in your vocabulary?' he continued silkily.

'I'm in no doubt it features in yours,' she said tartly, 'although it's spelt S-E-X, right?'

'Ouch.' He smiled, a lazy, sexy smile, before saying, 'I rather walked into that one, didn't I? You don't trust me an inch, do you, my fiery little puritan?'

She didn't like the 'puritan' bit; she wasn't sure if she liked the 'fiery' bit either if it came to it—it suggested a lack of control, and that wasn't at all the image she wanted to present to him. She took a long, silent pull of air, counted to ten, and then said sweetly, 'I'm sure you're an absolutely trustworthy employer, Mr Mallen,' before walking smartly to the door. 'Shall we bring up my things?'

He was grinning as he followed her out of the flat and

down the stairs, and as she caught sight of his face she tried, desperately, to hang on to the anger and hurt—it was all the protection she had—but it was difficult. He was so seductive when he was like this, and although she knew he was a virtuoso in the seduction techniques it was head knowledge, not heart, and didn't help at all against that magnetic pull he exerted as naturally as breathing.

'I'll take your cases up and leave you to get settled in,' Hawk said as they reached the car. 'There's a few phone calls I need to make.'

'Oh, but I thought we were going into the office?' She was flustered and it showed. 'I can just leave my things—'

'The day's over.' It was; dusk was already falling rapidly into the square, tingeing it with a bluey-grey softness, and there was the bite of frost in the air. 'I'm going to call in and inform Antoinette of the new arrangements, make those calls, and then pick up some bare essentials for you on my way back to my hotel. Okay? One day is going to make no difference one way or the other, Joanne. Go up, unpack, have a bath and relax until you hear my knock.'

'Hawk, there's no need; I can pop out myself—'

'Just do it, Joanne, will you?' he said with pointed weariness. 'You won the major battle today; you've chosen your accommodation and established you are an independent, tenacious free spirit and I am suitably humbled. Rest on your laurels.'

He didn't look humble—in fact the word was ludicrous when applied to Hawk Mallen, Joanne thought wryly—but he had made his point and she nodded quietly. 'All right. Thank you.'

She saw the dark eyebrows rise sardonically at her meekness and fought against smiling. She couldn't afford to soften in any way, shape or form; this was a battle, and she was fighting as much against herself and her weakening emotions where this man was concerned as against Hawk himself. He was just so dangerous, fascinatingly, hypnotically dangerous, and utterly ruthless in his desire to conquer, and if he ever had an inkling of the true state of her feelings for him... The thought propelled her into the house ahead of him and up the stairs as though the devil himself were after her.

Once alone amid her strewn possessions, Joanne stopped for a moment in her unpacking as she caught sight of herself in the bedroom mirror, noting the tension frown that marred her forehead.

Hawk was right; once she finished unpacking the first thing on the agenda was a hot bath, and she could wash her hair, change, spoil herself a little. He wouldn't be back for at least a couple of hours and the headache that was beginning to drum at the back of her eyelids needed soaking away. She nodded at the serious-faced girl in the mirror.

And once Hawk had dropped a few provisions off she'd fix something light to eat with a hot drink, and probably take it to bed with one of the books she'd brought with her from England. A nice relaxing night in her new home... She glanced round the pretty room in varying shades of lemon and ivory before leaving the suitcases and walking through to the sitting room again. She had been right to insist on moving from that first apartment, she told herself with a feeling of deep relief. She could be herself here, in this little oasis from the pressures that would undoubtedly come her way as Bergique & Son's new manageress. In fact she could have been happy—if only a certain tall, blue-eyed individual hadn't blazed on her horizon like a threatening black meteor.

*   *   *

The threatening black meteor was back at just gone seven, his arms full of groceries and his face—although she didn't like the tender pang that accompanied the thought—grey with tiredness.

Joanne, on the other hand, had bathed, washed her hair and spent a contented hour or two arranging her belongings before crashing out in front of the TV. The resulting feeling of guilt was overpowering, and when he placed the bags in the kitchen, remarking as he did so, 'There's a couple of bottles of good wine in that lot, and steaks and so on,' her following words were inevitable.

'Would...would you like to stay for a meal?' she asked hesitantly.

'Great.' It was immediate and satisfied, and although she knew he had set the whole thing up she couldn't be angry. He *did* look exhausted, and if she had accepted the first apartment he would be back in England now, so it was all her fault...in a way. 'I'll open the wine, shall I?' he asked with suspicious meekness that only confirmed the whole exercise had been planned.

'What about the car, the driver?' She gestured at the window to the square outside. 'Aren't you going to tell him?'

'I came by taxi.' His eyes glinted wickedly.

'And you didn't think to ask it to wait?' she murmured sarcastically. 'How fortunate I suggested you stay.'

'I had faith in your compassion.' He smiled slowly. 'Where's the corkscrew?'

She gave up. He couldn't be shamed; she should have known—he was impossible!

'Here.' She opened a drawer and gave him the corkscrew. 'But it's just dinner, okay? I'm as tired as you are and I need my bed.'

'I need your bed, Joanne,' he said, with a ridiculously lewd expression that was supposed to make her laugh.

It did, but it also sent her heart thudding as a cold clear warning hit her brain. Don't forget, he's never more dangerous than when he's amusing and charming, like now. You've no defence against this man but he doesn't know that, so play it cool and keep things easy.

The red wine was mellow and fruity, the sort that tasted of a thousand summer days and must have cost a small fortune. With Hawk perched on a breakfast stool watching her while she worked, preparing a salad to go with the steaks, Joanne consumed two glasses without even being aware of it, until her head became a little muzzy and she found herself giggling at something he said.

'I think I need some food.' She took a couple of raw mushrooms and popped them into her mouth, one by one. 'What on earth's in that wine anyway?'

'Just grapes and sugar and—'

'You know what I mean,' she admonished gravely. 'You aren't trying to get me tipsy, are you?'

'Would I?' The sapphire-blue eyes were laughing at her and it should have mattered—but it didn't.

She nodded solemnly, but then, in the next moment, he had taken the salad bowl and set it to one side, folding her into his body without saying a word.

Joanne's mistake was in opening her mouth to protest, because he simply seized the chance to plunder it, his tongue sending tremors of desire into every nerve and sinew.

He had already taken off his jacket and tie, his shirt open at the neck, and as her palms pressed against his chest she could feel the prickle of dark body hair under the silk and the combination was unbearably erotic.

'You're beautiful, Joanne, just beautiful,' he whispered softly as his mouth nibbled at her lower lip. 'You've no idea what you do to me.'

She had, oh, she had, if it was just a fraction of what he did to her, she thought helplessly.

'I could eat you alive, do you know that?' His mouth moved to her earlobe and she thought she would die. 'Every single inch of you.' His hand covered her breast, caressing it slowly through the thin cotton of the T-shirt she had changed into, and immediately the tip flowered beneath his expert fingers, aching and ripe.

She arched against him, her hands going up to his shoulders as she pressed herself against the hardness of his body, and then, as a sizzle and a splutter from the grill touched her senses, she jerked away, her voice agitated. 'The steaks! I can't burn the steaks on my first night here; what would Madame Lemoine think?'

'Damn Madame Lemoine.' But he let her move away and rescue the food, settling himself back on his stool as he purposefully poured them both another glass of wine, although Joanne determined not to have another drop until she had eaten.

They ate at the tiny dining-room table that was barely big enough for two, and Joanne made sure the third glass of wine lasted until dessert, a wonderful chocolate mousse piped with thick fresh cream that tasted divine.

'That was absolutely gorgeous.' She was licking her spoon clear of even the faintest trace of chocolate as she spoke and raised her eyes to see Hawk's narrowed gaze resting slumberously on her face.

'You look like a contented little cat,' he said huskily. 'I can almost hear you purr.'

'I love chocolate mousse,' she admitted with a faintly embarrassed smile. 'It's so decadent.'

'What else do you love, Joanne?' he asked softly. 'Do you realise I don't know the first thing about you besides the black and white information in your personnel folder? What music do you like? What books do you read? *Talk* to me.'

Talking was safer than not talking, and so she talked, guardedly at first, and then more freely after Hawk opened the second bottle of wine. And he responded in kind, telling her about his childhood, his youth, and then his desire to carve out a name for himself beyond that of Jed Mallen's grandson. The room was intimate and shadowed, lit only by the glow of the standard lamp in one corner, Hawk having turned the main light off before they ate, and Joanne was just thinking things were a sight too cosy for her peace of mind when Hawk said, 'Time I was making tracks.'

'What?'

His voice had been easy, cool, and she didn't feel like that; in fact she felt far from it. He had been leaning back in his seat for the last half an hour, his arms crossed over the broad expanse of his big muscled chest, and the open shirt collar displaying a hard tanned throat and the beginnings of black curling body hair. The silky material of his shirt seemed to emphasise rather than diminish his magnetic masculinity, and, try as she might, she had been struggling to dispel the thought of what he would look like without it for the last little while—and failing miserably. He looked darkly brooding, his Italian genes very much to the fore, and tough, and sexy, and...

'It's been a long day and you said you were tired,' he said softly.

She stared at him, trying to hide her irritation and ashamed of the resentment that had flared, hot and strong, at his offer to leave. He didn't want to kiss her. Well, that was fine, fine, she told herself silently; she would only have had to put him in his place if he had tried—whatever Hawk's place was. 'I am tired,' she agreed stiffly. 'Thank you for all the provisions you brought in; I really must pay you—'

'Don't be silly.' He interrupted her lazily, standing up and stretching like a powerful black beast of the forest, his piercing blue gaze never leaving her unknowingly vulnerable face that betrayed her confusion and hurt all too clearly. 'Look on it as a house-warming present if that makes you feel better. I only bought the bare essentials, by the way; the bulk of the order will be delivered some time after six tomorrow so make sure you're back by then.'

'Yes, I will, thank you…' He really *was* going to go, she thought numbly as she watched him reach for his jacket and shrug it over his broad shoulders, slipping his tie into one of the pockets as he did so. Whatever she had expected it wasn't this.

Hawk knew that, and his voice was an easy drawl as she walked with him to the front door. Tonight was not the night, much as his aching loins tried to persuade him differently. She had opened up more than he had expected, but she was still like a nervous doe, ready to bolt before the hunter.

When he took her—and he *would* take her—it would be with her full capitulation, mental and physical, and she would want him as much as he wanted her. He didn't question why her absolute surrender was so important to him, and his goodnight kiss was long and unhurried, his hand tender as it cupped her jaw and the gentle eroticism of his mouth controlled and determined.

'Goodnight, Joanne.' When he lifted his head she was trembling. 'The car will pick you up at eight in the morning.' And then he was gone.

CHAPTER SEVEN

JOANNE didn't know whether to be relieved or disappointed nine hours later when Hawk phoned, at seven in the morning, to say he was on his way to the States to deal with an emergency that had arisen in one of the Mallen subsidiaries. He wished her well in the new job, told her he would be in touch at some point to discuss how things were going, and that was that.

She put down the phone with a feeling of disbelief. So... Her restless night, the agitation at the prospect of seeing him that morning which had had her up and eating breakfast before six, had all been for nothing. He had happily upped and gone.

She sat down suddenly on one of the chairs and gave herself a thorough talking-to. Why shouldn't he just go? He was her employer, that was all, and he had done what was necessary and introduced her to her new staff. There was no reason for him to stay another hour in France— *not one*—and the last person he was answerable to was her. She was just glad—fiercely, overwhelmingly glad— that nothing of any significance had happened last night. His actions this morning only proved, beyond doubt, that all her misgivings were spot-on, she told herself miserably.

She was ready and waiting for the car at eight, and the flow of angry adrenalin that had begun with Hawk's cool voice that morning continued to flow all day, working to her advantage as she consumed vast quantities of data and had Antoinette, and the rest of the somewhat lethargic office staff, scurrying about like headless chickens. It was clear that the lackadaisical listlessness that

118

Pierre had allowed to take hold had permeated the entire firm, and also that certain members of the staff didn't appreciate having their cosy little world shaken to its foundations, Antoinette for one.

She was just considering taking the sulky French girl to task in spite of it being their first day together, having asked, three times in quick succession, for a folder which still wasn't forthcoming, when she looked up from her desk to see a tall, heavily built, floridly handsome man in the open doorway, his dark eyes fixed on her face.

'You must be Joanne Crawford?' He spoke before she had the chance to open her mouth, his English almost perfect and accentless. 'I am Pierre Bergique, Miss Crawford, and I must beg your forgiveness for not being here to introduce you to my staff personally yesterday.' He smiled, a wide crocodile kind of smile which didn't reach the hard, calculating black eyes. 'I trust Antoinette is looking after you in my absence?' he asked smoothly.

'Good morning, Pierre.' Hawk had warned her to start exactly as she meant to carry on with this man, and she saw the advice was apt as the toothy smile dimmed a little at her cool response. She couldn't allow him to relegate her to an underling—as his carefully worded greeting had aimed to do—neither could she acquiesce to the notion that he had authority over the staff any more. Pierre knew his position full well, and he was damned lucky not to be in a prison cell at this very moment, she thought tightly.

She rose with measured aplomb, walking round the desk and across the room before she held out her hand and said, 'How nice to meet you…at last. I'm sure things are going to work out splendidly, and rest assured I shan't hesitate to call on your services if I need to.'

Cold black eyes held determined honey-brown ones for a long—a very long—moment, and then Pierre took her hand, raising it to his lips and lightly kissing it before saying, his voice oily now, 'Charmed, charmed, my dear. I had no idea our intrepid new leader would prove to be quite so young and beautiful. Hawk must have been very impressed by your…capabilities.'

'Thank you.' It was all she could do not to whip her hand from his and rub the back of it to erase the feel of his fleshy lips, but she forced herself to smile and wait for a few seconds, ignoring the veiled innuendo in the barbed words, before turning away.

'I understand you will be working from home now, Pierre,' she said calmly as she re-seated herself, hoping the thudding of her heart wasn't making itself known. 'I would prefer that you check with me in the future before you call by so that I can make sure I'm available for you, and avoid wasting your time.'

Hawk had made it clear to Pierre that the offices were out of bounds beyond the occasional visit expected of a figurehead, and the clearing of his debts and the generous salary he was receiving each month for doing nothing were conditional.

'Of course.' It was too quick and too congenial. 'Anything you say.'

She didn't trust him an inch. 'Good.' She forced another smile but her flesh was creeping. This was one ugly customer, Joanne thought grimly, despite the façade of expensive clothes, well-groomed exterior and handsome, smiling countenance. This man could be nasty— she had seen too many like him in her working life to doubt her gut feeling—and she could understand Hawk's insistence that Pierre was virtually barred from crossing the firm's threshold now, although she had thought him a trifle hard when he had first told her.

'Perhaps you would allow me the pleasure of taking you to lunch one day?' The charm was out in full force, but it was too late; she had seen the man behind the mask and they both knew it.

'Thank you but I'm going to be busy for the next little while getting everything together,' Joanne said politely. 'Maybe after then?' Again they both knew there would be no lunch.

'Of course; just let me know when it will be convenient,' Pierre murmured with silky synthetic civility. 'And now you really must excuse me—a previous appointment...

Joanne breathed a sigh of relief when the door closed behind him, her body deflating in the chair like a punctured balloon. What a creep, but a crafty, astute creep, which also made him dangerous, and that was what she had to remember. He had been fooling people for years until Hawk had come on the scene and spoilt his little games; she had to be on her guard and take nothing for granted.

The next few weeks were challenging, frustrating, exhausting, at times stimulating and other times disappointing, but despite the hard, grinding work, long hours and mental and physical tiredness Joanne welcomed the pace. It made her so numb, so exhausted by the end of the day that all she could do was fall into bed and slip into a deep, dreamless sleep, sometimes without even having eaten her evening meal. But she could keep her thoughts away from Hawk and that was the main thing.

Sometimes she awoke, at the shrill command of her militant alarm clock, with his name on her lips and the faint recollection of shadowed memories buried deep in her subconscious, but mostly she could steel herself to deal solely with the job in hand, and she was glad of it.

He had rung two or three times a week since she had been in France, and she always came off the phone a quivering heap and desperately thankful he couldn't see how the sound of his deep, husky, totally male voice affected her.

Useless to tell herself he was ringing purely to see how the Mallen investment was progressing, that she meant nothing to him, that she was one of dozens, *hundreds*, of women whom he would invite to share his bed if he felt so inclined. She heard his voice and she melted; it was as simple—and as humiliating—as that.

So in the middle of November, on a particularly foul Friday when the rain was slashing at the windows of her office and nothing had gone right, she viewed the apparition in her office doorway as a figment of her fevered imagination and nothing else. Until it spoke, that was.

'Busy?'

Busy? She stared at Hawk as her brain struggled to respond. He was lounging against the open door, big and dark in a heavy leather jacket and black jeans, which were as different from the designer business suits he normally wore as chalk from cheese. The sight of him stopped her breath.

She forced herself to talk, to say *something*. 'I didn't know you were coming.'

'Neither did I until this morning.' He didn't move or smile.

She waited for him to elaborate, and, when he didn't, rose quietly from behind her desk, setting her face in a polite smile of welcome befitting a humble employee greeting the illustrious head of the Mallen Corporation. 'It's nice to see you again; is there anything specific you want to see me about?' she asked quietly.

'Don't tempt me, Joanne.' The look in his eyes was so blatant, and so sexual, that she blushed hotly as she held out one small hand for him to shake, and when he simply took her fingers in his and drew her close for a moment, his eyes roaming over her face before he kissed her lips in a light stroking movement that was over as soon as it had begun, she was still too stunned at his sudden appearance to offer any resistance.

'So...' He stepped back a pace, watching her with glittering eyes. 'Have you missed me?' he asked with the Mallen arrogance.

'Missed you?' How could he get so instantly under her skin? she asked herself angrily. 'Of course not.'

'Liar.' It was said matter-of-factly but still grated unbearably, tightening her mouth and narrowing her eyes.

'Hawk, I'm here to work and work I have,' she declared firmly. 'What on earth makes you think I've missed *you*?'

'Because it's impossible for me to have been feeling the way I have without you feeling something similar.' It was so surprising, and so unexpected, revealing as it did the man beneath the cool, arrogant exterior, that she just stared at him without saying anything. 'I've been sleeping you, eating you, tasting you,' he said softly. 'It's driving me nuts, Joanne. Every time I shut my eyes at night there's a slender titian beauty there, with honey-gold eyes and the sort of figure that makes a man ache.'

'Hawk—'

'It makes *me* ache—hell, how it makes me ache,' he murmured huskily. 'I'm in and out of that damn shower all night.'

'You're talking about sexual attraction—'

'I know; believe me, I know,' he agreed with a sardonic lift of his eyebrows.

'And I'm sure a man of your considerable experience could easily find a number from his little black book to take care of things,' she continued firmly, as though he hadn't interrupted. She was *not* going to be swept back into his orbit and then discarded so abruptly again; she just wasn't.

'Perhaps I haven't got a little black book?' he suggested softly.

'And perhaps pigs fly?' Joanne said sweetly, desperately glad the trembling in her stomach hadn't communicated itself to her voice.

'You think I'm the worst sort of philanderer, don't you?' It was a statement, not a question. 'And after I've been so restrained too,' he added sadly.

'Huh.' She had seen the wickedly amused glitter in the sapphire eyes and she wasn't fooled.

'Enough of this sparkling repartee.' He grabbed her suddenly, lifting her up and swinging her round as he kicked the door shut. 'You're going to spend the weekend with me.' It was another statement rather than an invitation.

'*I am not.*' It was hard to think while held close to his big masculine body, but the answer was instinctive anyway. He looked so good, he smelt so good, she wouldn't *dare* spend time with him.

'Reconsider.' He kissed her again, but this time it was no brief salutation but a long, deep, hard invasion that sent every nerve and sinew into overdrive. She found her arms snaking up to his broad shoulders and had to clench her fingers to restrain them, determined not to give in to the quivering hot excitement. 'Please?' he added softly as he lifted his head.

'No, I'm here to work——'

'Not at the weekends; even the wicked slave-driver Hawk Mallen doesn't expect that. Besides, you've been working too hard,' he said with sudden seriousness. 'You've lost weight, you look drawn.'

'Oh, thank you so much,' she muttered sarcastically, trying to pull away but knowing she wouldn't have any effect on the steel-hard arms. So he didn't like the way she looked now?

'But even more beautiful,' he added gently, his mouth twisting with amusement at her reaction. 'You have an ethereal quality now, as though a breath of wind would blow you away.'

'Hawk, let *go* of me.' She turned her head towards the door, worried Antoinette and the rest of the office staff would wonder why the door was shut, or, worse still, knock and walk straight in. Antoinette would make a meal of such a tasty titbit.

'Not till you agree to spend the weekend with me,' he said firmly. 'I can stay like this all afternoon; I'm enjoying it.' There was swollen evidence to prove he meant what he said, his hard body stirring against the soft swell of her stomach even as he spoke, and making her legs feel weak at his alien masculinity.

'What...what do you mean by "spend the weekend"?' she asked breathlessly, fighting against the urge to arch against his maleness, and then betraying her arousal helplessly with a tiny moan as one large hand stroked a sensual path from her throat to her waist, lingering possessively on the swell of one ripe breast.

'I want to show you France, my suspicious little siren.' He moved her slightly from him in order to look down into her flushed face. 'Although I can be persuaded otherwise,' he added softly. 'My hotel room has the biggest double bed you've ever seen—'

'*Hawk.*'

'Okay, okay.' His eyes crinkled as he gave the devastating smile he used so rarely, and she felt the impact right down to her toes. 'I promise I'll behave; how about that? No petting, no lovemaking—just a weekend spent in each other's company. I'm leaving for the States again first thing Monday morning and I know the next couple of weeks are going to be the very devil. I just wanted to be with you, Joanne; that's the top and bottom of it.'

It might have been calculated, he might be being manipulative again, but she couldn't struggle against the overwhelming desire to be with him when he looked at her like that. And he *had* promised...

'All right.' She felt such a burst of happiness that she

wanted to press herself into him and pull his head down to hers, and to fight that impulse she quickly stepped back a pace, purposely forcing his hands to drop to his sides. 'But a promise is a promise,' she warned shakily. 'And you've promised no lovemaking.'

'And you'll keep me to mine, no doubt,' he drawled wryly. 'I always thought women were the weaker sex, but since meeting you I've had to change my mind. I certainly chose well in Bergique & Son's new manager; if you deal with Pierre half as sternly as you deal with me, the poor guy won't know what's hit him.'

It was said mockingly, his eyes laughing at her, but a little chill crept into her heart as she turned away towards her desk. She wanted to be with him because she loved him; it might be foolish, crazy, but that was how it was. But Hawk? Hawk didn't know the meaning of the word love, and she forgot that at her peril. He wanted her body, he perhaps wanted an agent in the nest of vipers he had uncovered too, but anything permanent, with any sort of future? No chance.

The weekend began on the Friday night with a wonderful wander through the colourful streets, boulevards and cobblestone lanes, under a dark moonlit sky that had banished even the smallest rain cloud. The beautiful city, with its hundreds of statues, museums, countless churches, fountains and squares, narrowed down to one tall, dark, handsome man for Joanne, and a pair of piercingly blue, riveting eyes. Everything else faded into oblivion.

They ate at one of the many restaurants dotted around the streets of the gourmet capital, where taste, like the other senses, was taken so seriously. The restaurant was small and nondescript from the outside, and the interior wasn't much better, but the food was out of this world.

They feasted on *crudités variées*, a mixture of raw

vegetables with oil and vinegar, followed by steak *au poivre* which melted in the mouth, and was ably enhanced by the excellent champagne Hawk had ordered. The dessert—*un mystère*, which turned out to be vanilla ice-cream with meringue in the middle and chopped nuts on the outside—was perfect to follow the steak, and when Joanne accepted a second helping Hawk couldn't hide his surprise at her appetite.

'You said I was too thin,' she reminded him drily as she lifted her spoon and prepared to attack the delicious concoction. 'You ought to be pleased.'

'I am, oh, I am,' he assured her gravely, 'but I did not say you were too thin. You looked weary, that was all.'

Weary? Heart-sore, bone-achingly sad, perhaps, she thought painfully. 'I'm fine.' She beamed at him, determined to give nothing away. 'It's just been hectic, that's all, and I've needed to be fully alert at all times.' But never so much as now. 'There are one or two things I need to discuss with you, incidentally; we are going to have to reschedule—'

'Not now.' He interrupted her with a lazily raised hand that was none the less authoritative. 'The weekend is ours; Monday morning is soon enough for you to once again become the super-efficient career woman Bergique & Son know and love.'

'I don't know about the love,' she said wryly. Over the last few weeks she had been pleased to discover she was being treated with respect—grudging respect in some quarters—by her staff, and there were several now whom she liked, and who she felt liked her, but it had been an uphill struggle.

Since the incident with Pierre in her office, Antoinette had fallen into line, the sulkiness disappearing as though by magic and the girl appearing, to all intents and purposes, to be fully committed to her new boss. But... And there was a big 'but', Joanne thought pensively. She didn't trust the beautiful French girl, not one little bit. The turn-around had been too quick and too complete—something smelt fishy.

'I said Monday morning is soon enough to think of work.' Hawk's voice was a little put out and Joanne suddenly realised she was staring into space, and that it was highly likely Hawk didn't have too many women do that in his presence. She was surprised she had, to be honest, but the creepy, goose-pimply unease she had been feeling for days, if not weeks, had momentarily intruded into the evening and absorbed her in its shadow.

'Sorry.' In view of all the humiliation and pain she had suffered through him she couldn't resist adding, 'I was daydreaming,' as she gave him a cheerfully innocent smile.

'Charming.' The sapphire gaze was penetrating, but he smiled back. 'You believe in keeping your men humble, is that it?'

Humble? *Hawk Mallen?* The raw sexuality and powerful aura didn't lend themselves to humbleness, she thought breathlessly as the devastating smile did its usual damage to her equilibrium. In fact you might as well have asked the fierce bird of prey from whom he had taken his name to be humble, as the big dark man watching her so closely.

'I don't have men in the plural,' she prevaricated sweetly, knowing her colour was high. 'As you well know.'

'And heartily approve of,' he said solemnly. 'I think one man is more than enough for you, and, funnily enough, I know just the man...'

That evening was the beginning of the most wildly happy two days she had ever known, and, amazingly,

Hawk kept his promise—apart from the odd lingering kiss he assured her didn't count.

He picked her up from her apartment on Saturday morning very early, but already the November day was promising that the rain of the last week was a thing of the past, as it allowed a cold but bright sunshine to bathe everything in its light.

The sports car Hawk had hired for the weekend was lean and low and fairly ate up the miles as it headed towards the medieval majesty of Burgundy, passing Cistercian abbeys, dignified towns of stone, fortified hill-top villages and wonderful roaming countryside, on its way to Dijon.

They ate lunch at a charming little *hostellerie*, and the toasted ham and cheese sandwiches, followed by bar-quettes au marron—pastry boats loaded with almond paste, chestnut cream, and sealed in with milk chocolate on one side and coffee icing on the other—were sublime. But anything would have tasted sublime—because she was with Hawk. And it frightened her. Frightened, ex-hilarated, excited, but mostly frightened. Because it would end. It had to.

They reached Dijon just after one in the afternoon— Joanne having insisted they stop and wander round one of the towns on their way—and the once-capital of the Flemish-Burgundian state was at its regal best in the bright sunshine.

'An afternoon of improving your mind?' Hawk asked lazily, after they had parked at the edge of a delightfully ancient little market-place, where Hawk bought them both the most enormous ice-creams. 'We can visit the Musée des Beaux-Arts, and perhaps you would like to see the Well of Moses? It is a very powerful sculpture, very moving.'

'Is it?' She licked a blob of strawberry ice-cream from the corner of her mouth, and Hawk's eyes followed her

pink tongue, his gaze slumberous and hot. She was looking at a real flesh-and-blood sculpture that would knock
the Well of Moses into a cocked hat, Joanne thought
silently, with an irreverence that would have made Claus
Sluter turn in his grave. 'I don't mind what we do.'

'A submissive *and* beautiful woman... My cup run-
neth over,' Hawk drawled mockingly.

Later that evening, after they had dined at the elegant
and luxurious hotel where Hawk had reserved rooms—
'Two singles,' he had emphasised sadly as they had
sipped their pre-dinner cocktails. 'Now, I deserve some
credit for that at least, Joanne—' He suggested a walk
in the beautifully landscaped gardens that were lit as
brightly as day with hundreds upon hundreds of tiny
swinging lanterns.

She stared at him warily. From what she had seen of
the gardens earlier that evening as they had watched a
sunset that was all vermilion, glowing mauve and deep-
est rose-gold, they were the epitome of a romantic stroll
for two—complete with hidden bowers, tiny fountains
and the inevitable love-seats dotted about the most intimate corners.

'I don't know...' The mellow, incomparable wines of
the region, two of which she had imbibed pretty freely
at dinner, were not conducive to good control.

'Well, I do.' He solved her dilemma by taking her
hand and drawing her up from her seat, and again she
found herself relishing the power, the authority, the sheer
masculinity in his lean, strong frame, which had drawn
the eyes of more than one predatory female during their
meal.

And she knew what most of them were thinking. Why,
why, is he with her? But he was, and it was her he had
asked to walk with him...

This intoxicating thought carried her out into the gardens in something of a smug daze, but as the cool night air stroked her face, its warning caress carrying the scent of starry, frost-touched nights, cold reason asserted itself.

Her mother had been the sort of woman who had allowed men to use her, time after time after time, and then walk away when they had had enough. She didn't know if her mother had loved these men—she had certainly felt more for them than she had her own flesh and blood, that was for sure—but there had been something, some elemental driving desire to be loved, that had proved weakening and dangerous. Could those sorts of things be passed on in the genes?

As Hawk tucked one of her arms in his, the strength and bulk and smell of him overwhelmingly intoxicating, her mind raced on.

She *knew* he couldn't—or wouldn't—accept the concept of a monogamous lifestyle, that he didn't want to even try. She was a passing whim with him, perhaps a challenge that had stirred his jaded appetite for a while, added to which her usefulness at Bergique & Son couldn't be ignored. In fact—and here her mind balked a little as she made herself face the truth—he was a loner, a man who answered to no one, kept his own counsel and liked it that way. He would never settle down, he just wasn't the type, and that was exactly—*exactly*—the sort of man her mother had been inexplicably drawn to, despite all rhyme and reason, in the same way a moth was drawn to the bright light that would ultimately spell its destruction.

'What are you thinking about?'

His voice was soft and deep, and its very gentleness made her speak before she considered her words. 'My mother, actually,' she said quietly.

'Do you miss her?' There was no shred of surprise in

the calm voice, although it couldn't have been the answer he was expecting.

'Not in the way you mean; she wasn't that sort of
mother,' Joanne said with painful honesty.

They had walked into a part of the garden that was
almost Victorian in its layout, very sheltered and pretty,
and now, as he drew her down on to a lacy wooden seat,
it felt as though they were the only two people alive in
all the world. The night was breathtakingly still, not a
sound from the hotel in the distance disturbing the tranquillity, and when Hawk said, 'Tell me about her, about
you, about your childhood,' the strange, almost dream-
like quality of the night loosened her tongue.

He was a good listener—too good—and when she fell
quiet, some twenty minutes later, it was with the realisation she had said far more than she intended.

'I'm sorry, Joanne.' And he was, and also murder-
ously angry with the woman who had borne her and then
cast her aside at such a young, vulnerable age. The anger
he was trying to hide made his voice grim, hard even,
and she cast a quick troubled glance at him before looking straight ahead again.

'It's all right,' she said stiffly. He was annoyed with
her for going on the way she had, she thought wildly.
She shouldn't have said all that—she couldn't believe
she had; he had probably just wanted a few light facts
about her early life, not an in-depth year-by-year account. He must think she was pathetic—

'No, no, it isn't,' he said flatly, still in the same forbidding voice. 'Every child should know it's loved and
wanted.'

'Were you?' She wouldn't have dared to ask normally, but here it seemed right, and she wanted to turn
the conversation from her.

'Loved and wanted? Very much,' he said quietly. 'My
mother...my mother was the sort of person who lived to

make others happy, and her whole life revolved around my father and me, and her friends. You could say she was her own worst enemy.'

'By loving her family?' Joanne protested.

'By caring too much—for my father at least.' He raked a hand through his short black hair. 'She never revealed, by one word or action, the misery he inflicted upon her. She simply fought through every day of her life trying to make things right that could never be right. I can't accept that sort of emotion can be called love—it is obsession, the most damaging sort of obsession.'

'You're saying that simply because you can't handle the fact that love exists,' Joanne said quietly. 'Perhaps she considered that the good times she had with him were worth all the pain and anguish.'

'Then she was a fool.' The words were dragged out of the depths of him, his voice harsh and jagged. 'Just as your mother was a fool. And I still think that what my mother felt for my father, and your mother felt for her husbands and lovers, was obsession, not love. I can't accept—' He stopped abruptly, a muscle clenching at the side of his jaw, before he said, 'What the hell? None of it matters in the long run.'

'Hawk—'

'I'll show you what's real one day, Joanne.' His voice was savage and cold, and made his following words all the more chilling. 'I'll make love to you until nothing and no one exists, until the earth melts away and all you can see and hear and touch is me. I shall kiss every inch of your body, see you mindless beneath me, begging for what only I can give you. And you'll want me—you'll want me so badly you'll be on fire—but we'll both know exactly what we are doing.'

'And it won't mean anything?' she asked faintly, caught up in his blackness.

'Of course it will mean something.' He caught her

face in his hands, his eyes urgent now and the terrible anger fading. 'It will mean one hell of a lot but we won't be fooling ourselves, don't you see? You are a casualty of your mother's obsession with this fantasy called love—'

'No, I don't want to hear this.' She jerked away from him, her voice shaking. This was all wrong; he had twisted everything to make it all wrong but she couldn't find the words to tell him...

'Shh. Shh, now.' Suddenly he was tender, frighteningly tender, folding her into his big hard frame and holding her close to his heart for a long moment, before lowering his head and taking her trembling mouth in a kiss that was pure enchantment. 'So fierce and so brave, so beautiful...' His voice was a soft caress against her lips and she couldn't fight it—or him.

One moment he was fire and brimstone, the next fiercely tender, and the effect was hypnotic. She didn't understand him—she didn't have a clue what went on in that ruthless male mind, and perhaps it didn't matter anyway, so long as he didn't guess the state of her true feelings towards him. Because one day soon his desire for her would wane, when someone else more suitable caught his fancy, and that would be that. He would give up the chase, retire gracefully, and no doubt allow the new lady the pleasure of licking his wounds.

He explored her mouth slowly, taking his time, and her bones dissolved into a warm, aching throb before he raised his head again.

'You're still holding me to that promise?' His voice was dry, very dry, and she just knew he knew she wanted to say no.

She nodded. The tumult of sensuous pleasure his lips had induced was not conducive to clear speech, and she didn't intend to give him the satisfaction of hearing her shaky whisper.

'Pity.' He bent and kissed the tip of her nose before pulling her to her feet. 'Great pity...' he drawled easily, his mouth drawn to hers again in a searching, lingering kiss that sent waves of pleasure right down to her toes, before he lifted his head and slipped an arm round her waist as they began to walk down the secluded little path again.

He could kiss, he could *really*, *really* kiss, she thought fretfully, desperately hoping her trembling hadn't been noticed by that wicked narrowed gaze. But then, he'd had plenty of practice, hadn't he? It was easy for him to remain controlled, cold even.

And why, *why* had she told him all that about her childhood, let him in like that, when she knew he wasn't really interested and would view it exactly as he had, with barely concealed contempt?

'Is that the first time you've shared with anyone about your mother?' The deep gravelly voice was quite expressionless, and, tucked into his side as she was, she couldn't see the look on his face to gauge how best to reply, and simply decided to go for the truth.

'Yes.' She paused a moment before continuing quickly, 'It simply hasn't cropped up before—'

'Now don't spoil it with a lie.'

'How dare you—?'

'I'm honoured you trusted me enough to tell me, Joanne.' He stopped, moving her round to face him as he held her within the circle of his arms, his face deadly serious and stopping all coherent thought in her head. 'I'm glad she's not around any more because I would have had a hard job to keep my hands off her, but...I'm glad you told me.'

No, don't; don't do this to me. She stared up at him, her honey-brown eyes wide and swimming with emotion. The fire and brimstone she could cope with, the ardent lover...possibly—certainly the ruthless, hard

businessman was a cinch—but this tender, quiet side of
him that she had seen over the last twenty-four hours
was something else. Something…devastating.

'Come on.' He moved them on again, and now there
was a wry quirk at the corner of the hard, firm mouth.
'Keep moving, my nervous little fawn, because when
you look at me like that I'm very tempted to do something I've never done before in my life.'

'What?' she asked nervously.

'Break a promise.'

Joanne awoke the next morning with her heart singing
and her pulse racing at the thought of another whole day
with Hawk. She gave herself a stern talking-to in the
shower, and again when she was drying her hair and
getting dressed in black leggings, high black boots and
a long baggy cream jumper, but the singing remained.

She loved him. Utterly, completely—against all the
odds and every grain of common sense, she loved him.
And she was going to take this last day of the magical
weekend—which would probably never be repeated—
and *enjoy* it.

They left Dijon after breakfast to travel southwards
towards the time-mellowed villages of Provence, the de-
lightful contrasts of southern France adding to the enchantment of the day. Hawk made for Cassis, a pictur-
esque fishing village on the coast, where they enjoyed a
delicious alfresco lunch of freshly caught crab sitting on
the verandah of a seafood restaurant, with the weak
November sun warming their heads while they ate.

The afternoon was spent strolling round the capital of
Provence, Aix-en-Provence, and visiting the fine cathe-
dral, although Joanne noticed very little beyond the tall,
dark man at her side. She was falling more and more in
love with him—she couldn't help it—and it scared her
half to death, making the time bittersweet.

It was late afternoon and they were walking along a road bordering a gracious square, when Joanne noticed two small children with their noses pressed against a shop window, watching a clockwork Santa Claus filling his sledge with toys. The laughing little tots were enraptured, their mother standing indulgently to one side as she smiled at their rosy faces, and as they passed she nodded at them and they nodded back, although Joanne felt her face had frozen.

'What is it?'

She hadn't thought Hawk had noticed, and now she tried to prevaricate as she said, her voice bright, 'I'm sorry?'

'Something in that little scene back there upset you. Why?' He stopped dead, turning her round to face him and looking down into her eyes, his gaze piercingly intent as he repeated, 'Why, Joanne?'

'I don't know what you mean.' *Enough.* Enough soul-baring for one weekend, she thought desperately as she stared back up at him, so big and dark and handsome in his black leather jacket and black jeans. Tomorrow morning, or the next day, he would be gone—probably for weeks, maybe for months—and she wanted to get through this weekend with nothing but pleasant memories to look back on.

Whenever they parted, whatever the circumstances, she was always left feeling vulnerable and broken, and she didn't want that this time. She had to master this overwhelming longing to draw close to him, to lower her defences and let him in, because it wouldn't mean to Hawk what it meant to her. He didn't *understand* what this exposure of her innermost self was costing her.

'Yes, you do.' He wasn't going to let it go; she could read his determination in the set of his mouth and narrowing of his eyes. 'Was it the children? Was that it? Or—'

'No, it wasn't the children,' she said quietly, horrified at the possibility he might think she was neurotic about children and families after her revelations the night before. 'They were sweet and their mother looked nice.'

'What, then?' he persisted softly. 'Tell me; I want to know.'

'I just don't like Christmas, that's all.'

She made to walk on but he caught her arm as she moved out of the circle of his arms, swinging her back to face him, his brow furrowed with enquiry. 'When I say tell me, I mean *tell* me,' he said firmly. 'That wasn't an answer. Explain.'

'Hawk, I'm sorry, I don't mean to be rude, but why should I?' she said tightly, trying to hide the panic his insistence was causing. 'If I don't like Christmas it's no big deal, is it? Lots of people the world over find it one big headache—it's so commercial.'

'You're not lots of people,' he said softly. 'You're thatched country cottages with roses round the door and big fat tabby cats, you're roasting chestnuts and log fires, you're snowmen, and frosted spider webs and a hundred and one other things I could think of, so...' He paused, his eyes blue light. 'Why don't you like Christmas, Joanne? And don't give me the ''commercial'' garbage either.'

She stared at him helplessly, suddenly overwhelmed by the most awful feeling that she wanted to cry. She couldn't, she *couldn't*, she told herself fiercely. It would embarrass them both and there was no logical reason for it anyway; just because he'd said something nice... If it *was* nice—perhaps he meant she was predictable and boring? But he hadn't said it that way...

'Well?'

His voice was very gentle, and to combat the emotion that was causing a physical pain in her chest her own was almost harsh as she said, 'Christmas was always a difficult time when I was a child, that's all. The home…the home did its best, but it wasn't like family.'

From the age of nine, after her mother's disastrous second marriage had ended so abruptly, she had resided permanently in the children's Home with no more placements with foster parents, and it had been then that the full significance of her isolation had washed over her.

She had been dispatched back just two weeks before Christmas, confused and heartbroken at her mother's rage towards her, and had cried herself to sleep for the next few nights, longing for even a glimpse of her mother's face.

And then Christmas Eve had come, its mystery and wonder taking hold of her even through the turmoil and pain, and she had been sure, so sure, her mother would visit her. Why she had been so adamant she didn't know, even now, but only her mother could make everything all right, and how could she not come at Christmas? And so she had waited, and waited… And the long day had eventually drawn to a close, and still she had sat at one of the windows looking out into the snow-filled darkness, until one of the home's helpers had persuaded her to go to bed. It had been March before she saw her mother again…

'Don't look like that.' His voice was strained, and it brought her out of the black reverie with a peculiar little jolt, her eyes focusing on his face instead of the small, lost child in her mind.

'Like what?' she asked shakily, her face very pale.

'Crushed, defeated,' he said with a painful grimness. 'We will forget this conversation; I will not allow it to spoil what little we have left of the weekend.'

The tone of his voice stunned her even as she found it impossible to determine exactly how he was feeling, and the next moment he had swept her along the street, his arm about her waist, as they made for the car.

'We are going to have a wonderful meal—I know the very place—and then I am going to fly you back to your apartment in time for you to be tucked up with your cocoa and hot-water bottle before midnight.'

His voice was mocking and light, but as her feet were hardly touching the floor it was some moments before she could gasp, 'Fly? In the air, you mean?'

'Is there another way?'

'But how?' They reached the car and she leant against the smooth bonnet as she repeated, 'How, Hawk? I mean—'

'A friend of mine has a private airfield near here, and I told him we'd be along this evening,' Hawk said calmly, as though he were suggesting they call by and have coffee with someone. 'I do have a pilot's licence if that's what's worrying you.' He raised his eyebrows sardonically, thoroughly enjoying her open-mouthed surprise.

'But what about the car?' she asked weakly.

'It will be collected.'

How the other half lived. She stared at him with wide eyes, not sure of what to think. He clicked his fingers and the world snapped smartly to attention, doffing its cap as it did so. How could she imagine, even in her wildest dreams—and there had been a few of those since she had fallen in love with Hawk—that she could ever mean anything more to him than a passing pleasure?

As he opened the car door she slid inside with a careful smile, even as the pain in her heart caught her breath. The weekend was over. Reality was back.

CHAPTER EIGHT

DURING the next few weeks Joanne worked very hard, even harder than she had done before Hawk's flying visit. She arrived at the office long before the rest of the staff and was still there for hours after they had vanished into the chill of the winter evenings, often leaving well after nine o'clock when the nights were cold and dark and the moon sailed brightly in a lonely sky.

She welcomed the hard, grinding slog; it was a very necessary opiate against the agony of soul that gripped her if she allowed herself to think of Hawk—in fact she didn't think she could have got through those few weeks leading up to Christmas without it.

He had dropped her at her apartment on the Sunday evening of their weekend together with nothing more adventurous than a brief, but passionate, embrace, and a long, lingering kiss that had brought fire to her cheeks and pain to her heart.

The next morning at the office he had very definitely stepped into business mode, his manner cool and remote and the ruthless side of him to the fore as he had caused a miniature whirlwind of panic and confusion among the rest of the staff, who had spent the day running hither and thither in ever decreasing circles.

Everyone—including Joanne—had breathed a deep sigh of relief when he had flown back to England that same night, although the next day the office had seemed strangely dull and empty, and the hours endless. His phone calls since then had been spasmodic and often terse, and in the last few days approaching the holiday period her heart had finally accepted what her head had been trying to tell her for weeks—the celibate weekend had convinced him to leave her alone. And instead of the relief that would have been logical in the circumstances there was only a deep, dark, consuming blackness that ate away at her appetite, her sleep, everything that made up life.

She had to get the victory over this. As the taxi-cab whisked her home that night, three days before Christmas, Joanne looked at her wan reflection in the window and sighed heavily. She had enough on her plate as it was—the more she delved into the workings of Bergique & Son, the more she discovered just what a crook Pierre Bergique was and how many dubious deals he'd had going for him—and she just couldn't afford to be distracted by any sort of personal life.

Personal life? The phrase mocked her. Some personal life she had—on a par with the average nun, although if she had to put them side by side the nun would have her vote.

She sighed again, the icy drizzle outside the warmth of the cab clothing everything in a grey gloom that perfectly matched her mood. She wished she'd never stepped foot in France and taken on the daunting task of turning Bergique & Son round, she wished she'd followed her instinct and branched out into pastures new, without any threads from the past still clinging on to her; but most of all, *most of all*, she wished she'd never heard of Hawk Mallen.

She paid the driver and walked into the house with her head down and her mind a million miles away, and as she bumped into someone in the hall she was just going to apologise when her eyes met the piercing blue gaze that had haunted her for weeks.

'What time do you call this?' He sounded angry and irritated, and from one blinding moment of wild delight she plummeted into raw pain and hurt that he could care so little when she cared so much.

'Nearly ten o'clock,' she said crisply. 'What time do you call it?'

'Too damn late, that's what.' He glared at her, the sapphire eyes as cold as glass. 'I've got better things to do than sit here twiddling my thumbs while you gad about on a date.'

'A date?' Her senses were registering he looked gorgeous, totally drop-dead gorgeous, her fingers were itching to give him a good slap. 'What on earth are you talking about?'

'I'm talking about the reason you are so late home,' he said icily. 'Your hours are nine to four forty-five, and it is now—'

'I know what the darn time is,' she hissed furiously, longing to scream at him but knowing it would fetch Madame Lemoine out of her burrow like a bullet out of a gun. 'And not that it's any of your business, but I've been working, *working*, like I have done every other night I've been in this damn country. How do you think I've been getting the sort of results I have if I'd limited myself to a nine-to-five mentality? Answer me that! Or do you think I'm one of those females that sits about chatting on the phone all day and painting her toenails—?'

'Don't you mean fingernails?' he interjected with sudden and suspicious meekness.

'Fingernails, toenails—the thought's the same,' she bit back angrily. 'Besides which you've got no right to object one way or the other. You didn't tell me you were visiting France—'

'I had a fax sent this morning.'

'Well, I didn't receive it,' Joanne snapped tightly, 'and even if I had, and I'd made previous arrangements of some sort or other, I wouldn't have changed them.

You own my work time, Hawk, not the rest of me, so let's get that quite clear.'

'Clear it is.' The coldness had evaporated like the morning mist and pure Mallen charm had taken its place. 'Have you eaten?'

'Eaten?' The sudden switch in mood and conversation had lost her.

'Because if not I would suggest you do so and then get an early night. We're flying to the States tomorrow morning, and no doubt you'll want to be up with the lark.'

She nearly said, The States? in the same tone of voice she'd said, 'Eaten?' and stopped herself just in time, taking a deep calming breath before she spoke with a quietness she was proud of considering the circumstances. 'I have no more intention of flying to America in the morning than I have of allowing you to dictate what time I go to bed,' she said firmly. 'I don't know why you're here or what's wrong, but you're not bullying me like you do everyone else, Hawk.'

'My grandfather is worse.' The blue eyes were steady as they held her honey-brown gaze and watched it widen with shock and concern. 'He's expressed a wish to see you.'

'Me?' She stared at him in astonishment.

'You are now in charge of his old friend's pride and joy, Joanne,' Hawk said quietly. 'I would have thought it only natural he wants to see you for himself.'

'Oh, I see.' She didn't, not really; in fact it seemed crazy to request her presence in America when Jed Mallen could have all the relevant facts and figures as to how she was doing in a few moments of time thanks to modern technology. 'But I can't leave tomorrow. I'm sorry, but I just can't. I've things to do, people to see—'

'I thought you said you weren't involved with anyone here,' he said softly, his voice cold again.

'Business people, Hawk.' She glared at him before remembering he must be worried sick about his grandfather, and, making a conscious effort to moderate her tone, she continued, 'There's the matter of Netta Productions for a start. I'm supposed to meet the son of the ex-managing director tomorrow and I need to hear what he wants to say; he's sure his father was bankrupted deliberately—'

'Delegate.'

If he was trying to wind her up he was certainly succeeding, Joanne thought tightly as she struggled to keep any irritation from showing. Delegate indeed! 'It's not as simple as that, as well you know,' she said flatly. 'Surely your grandfather wouldn't mind if I saw him at the end of the month?'

'And what will you do over Christmas—work?' he asked with a curious lack of expression. 'Is that the way you take care of your particular ghosts, Joanne—by pretending they don't exist? Well, I'm sorry, we're flying tomorrow, and the return ticket is for December the twenty-ninth.'

'You mean stay over Christmas?' she asked weakly. 'Is that what you mean?'

'That's what I mean, Joanne,' he drawled mockingly, temper and aplomb apparently quite restored. 'Bergique & Son won't grind to a halt because you leave the helm briefly. If there's one thing I've learnt in life it's that no one is indispensable, however much they like to imagine they are.'

'I don't imagine anything—'

'I do.' Suddenly his eyes were blue fire, hot and sensuous. 'Hell, you wouldn't believe what I imagine...' He pulled her into his arms almost roughly. 'You're in my head, do you know that? Locked in there, all long legs and creamy smooth skin... You drive me crazy.'

He bent his head and his mouth was hungry on hers,

so hungry it lit an immediate flame in the core of her. She didn't want to respond to him; it wasn't *fair* that he could move in and out of her life like this, taking her up and then dropping her at will, but she might as well have tried to stop the rhythm of the tides as withstand him.

'I've thought about you every moment,' he whispered against her lips. 'Shy, beautiful Joanne. What is it about you that I can't get out of my mind?'

She opened her mouth to answer, to tell him that he couldn't fool her with all his sweet talk, but he took the words before they were uttered, his lips and his tongue probing as he folded her more deeply into him, wrapping his big dark overcoat round her as he enclosed them in a blanket of warmth.

'Say you'll come with me, Joanne.' She was utterly captivated by the time he raised his head again, lost in the flowing river of sensation that had turned her fluid. 'I want to spend some time with you, to show you my home, my friends. Say you'll come?'

This was a planned assault, an orchestrated campaign to get what he wanted, but even as the warning flashed through her mind she knew she was going to say yes. It was the gentleness that had done it, the languorous tenderness he had displayed that was so very un-Hawk-like and consequently terribly seductive.

'Well?' His voice was husky and deep. 'You'll say yes?'

'Would it make any difference if I said no?' she asked shakily, that tiny instinct in the back of her mind forbidding the total capitulation she longed to give. 'Would you take any notice?'

'You know I wouldn't.' He smiled, a wry little smile that crinkled the corners of his eyes. 'But it would be good for my ego to have you there with me instead of fighting every inch of the way.'

'Your ego needs help?' she asked disbelievingly, pulling away an inch or two to look more closely into the devastatingly attractive face.

'Around you, yes.' She couldn't read anything in his deadpan expression, the mask he was so good at adopting suddenly very firmly in place. 'But I'm a big boy now; I can take it,' he added with mocking dryness, before turning and walking with her still held within the circle of one arm to the stairs. 'I'll see you to your door.'

'There's no need.' She was trembling but she couldn't help it. Here, in the hall, with the possibility of Madame Lemoine or the other flat-dwellers liable to appear at any moment, she had had some protection. But upstairs...

'Joanne, I've been waiting for over four hours to see you; I'm tired, I'm hungry, and I was cold...until I held you in my arms, that is,' he said with wry self-derision at his all too obvious arousal, the alien power of which she had felt as he had held her close. 'I'm going to see you to your door, and then leave you to your chaste little bed, okay? I'm bushed too.'

She couldn't answer so she just nodded, the confession that the great Hawk Mallen, the powerful and authoritative figure who had the world at his fingertips and a reputation for ruthlessness that was second to none, had been waiting for four hours in the hall of a little French house to see *her* rendering her dumb.

'Goodnight, little fawn.' They had stopped outside her front door and he cupped her face gently, his eyes piercingly blue as they looked into hers. 'Hell, you're lovely...' This time the kiss was fierce and burningly hot as he slipped his hands beneath her open coat and under the soft wool of her waist-length jumper, his fingers encircling the soft swell of her breasts and branding her skin with heat. She could feel him shaking as his tongue penetrated the sweetness of her mouth, his body rock-hard against hers, and his heart slamming against his chest like a sledgehammer.

Her love for him, stimulated by the need he couldn't hide, was sending her up in flames and she found she was breathing his name as she kissed him back with ever increasing passion, her head swimming and a wild clamouring in her senses that caused her to press deeper and deeper into the powerfully muscled body against hers.

'Damn it, Joanne, another minute and I shan't be able to stop.' His voice was a low growl of frustration and need, and as he unwound her arms from round his neck she saw his control was paper-thin. 'And that would really blot my copy-book, wouldn't it?' he stated with grim amusement. 'Your body might be willing but there's still that hesitation in your eyes that tells me you don't trust me yet.'

'It's important that I trust you?' she asked shakily. Trust him? She'd die for him.

'Strangely, yes.' He stood looking down at her, his face shadowed and dark and his big body taut and still. 'Yes, it is. Get some sleep, Joanne, and I'll see you in the morning.' His voice was suddenly cool, almost remote, and he had turned on his heel and begun to walk down the stairs before she could reply.

Los Angeles was everything Joanne had expected and more, but the shock of Hawk's sudden appearance, added to the long plane journey and electric tension that was gripping every nerve and sinew, rendered her almost deaf, dumb and blind on their arrival on the balmy West Coast. She was aware of the pleasant temperature—after the icy drizzle they had left behind in Paris the warm soft air that resembled a mild spring day in England was wonderfully relaxing—but little else registered on the drive from the airport to Hawk's home in Beverly Hills, the mental and physical exhaustion that had been steadily building for the last few weeks paramount.

Hawk seemed to understand perfectly, taking care of her in the same way he did everything else—calmly, firmly and with absolute authority, so that she was whisked effortlessly from pillar to post almost without being aware of it.

As they drew up outside Hawk's mansion, Joanne's impression of high, impenetrable walls—the perimeter surround being ten feet high—was overtaken by one of light and colour and life as they left the car and walked to the open door, where a pretty little maid was waiting for them.

The hall was vast and dominated by the biggest Christmas tree Joanne had ever seen, a vision of gold and red, with antique golden baubles, stars and ribbons, tiny flickering red candles and gold-berried ivy, all of which matched the deep red sofas scattered about the lushly carpeted expanse. Several piles of ravishing gifts were stacked under the tree, wrapped up in shiny gold paper and tied with green and pistachio ribbons.

'It's beautiful.' Joanne's voice was a soft murmur but Hawk heard it, and also recognised the dazed, vacant note as being indicative of near collapse.

'And it will still be here tomorrow,' he said quietly, 'along with the rest of the house. For now it's bed for you.'

'What?' Even in her tired state the word 'bed', when spoken by Hawk Mallen, was not to be ignored. She hadn't quite summoned up the nerve to ask him what the sleeping arrangements for this little holiday extravaganza would be, and she still couldn't find the words, but it didn't matter. He had read her mind. As always.

'I'm sorry, Joanne, but you can't get your itchy little fingers on my body tonight,' he said sardonically, with a cool disregard for the listening maid that brought mor-

tifying colour flooding into Joanne's pale face. 'You'll
have your own suite while you are my guest; kindly see
that you stay in it without any midnight ramblings.'

'Hawk, that's not funny—'

'You're suffering from a combination of jet lag and
overwork,' he continued as though she hadn't spoken.
'Tomorrow you have the morning in bed, okay? And
Conchita will bring you a dinner tray once you've bathed
and slipped into bed tonight.'

'I'm not a child,' she protested quickly.

'Tell me about it.' He gave a theatrically leering
smile, his eyes laughing at her, and in spite of herself
she smiled back. He was impossible. Quite, quite impossible, and she loved him so much it scared her to
death.

Her suite was like something out of a Hollywood
movie, and made the first apartment that Hawk had chosen in France seem positively modest.

'Conchita will run you a long hot bath.' Hawk sig-
nalled to the maid as he spoke, who immediately dis-
appeared into the huge blue marble bathroom which
boasted a bath that would easily have accommodated a
team of rugby players. 'And while you're soaking she'll
unpack your things and turn the bed down. Ring when
you're ready for your meal; there's a bell-push over the
bed.'

'Right...thank you.' She was too exhausted to hide
the fact that she was completely overawed, her stance
very much like that of a tired and nervous child as she
stood just inside the luxurious blue sitting room after her
quick tour of the suite, unconsciously nipping at her
lower lip, her eyes shadowed with fatigue and apprehension.

'Come here.' His voice was very quiet, and as he
beckoned her to him in the middle of the room she
moved slowly to his side. 'It will all fall into place in

the morning, Joanne,' he said softly. 'Trust me in that if nothing else.' His arms were comforting as he pulled her against his broad chest, but the deliciously male smell of him, added to the muscled power of the big body, brought the quivery feeling snaking through her limbs, and after he had kissed her—lightly, as though she were a kid sister or maiden aunt, she thought testily—she stood quite still in the middle of the room as he left, not trusting her legs.

She cried in the bath once she was alone. How could she even begin to compete with the beautiful, sophisticated women he was used to? she asked herself miserably, lying back in the warm, scented water with her eyes shut as hot tears burnt a path down her cheeks. They would take this house in their stride, revel in it, live up to it, whereas she... She had never felt so like a fish out of water in her life—the outsider looking in. Even the worst times in the home couldn't compare to the misery that was swamping her right now.

It wasn't as though he had *chosen* for her to come here even. His grandfather had wanted to meet her and so she had been brought over like...like a package, a parcel, she thought desperately. That was all she represented to him—a commodity, a useful piece of equipment, a loyal employee— *Oh, stop it! Enough!* The words were caustic in her head as she realised, even in her anguish, she was going too far.

He liked her, he was physically attracted to her—that much she was sure about, whether she was versed in the arts of love or not. He would be only too pleased to have an affair with her; he'd made that plain too. Yes, there was no doubt he was genuine in his desire for her—the trouble was he didn't desire or like her enough for it to be love. And, loving him as she did, that made the whole situation a very definite checkmate. And neither of them won.

She stayed in the bath until the water was tepid, her aching muscles slowly relaxing as the silky warmth did its job, and after washing her hair she climbed out slowly, surprised at how leaden her legs felt. It was all she could do to slip into her nightie and towel-dry her hair, and the thought of drying it with the hairdryer was beyond her, so she left it damp about her neck as she slid into bed and rang for Conchita to bring her meal. Not that she really wanted to eat...

Only it wasn't the little maid who came into the room after a polite knock.

'Hawk!' She shot down in the bed, embarrassingly aware of the transparency of the nightie, her lack of make-up, her scraggy hair... 'What are you doing?'

'Bringing your meal—what else?' He walked across to the bed with casual animal grace, looking even more devastating than usual in charcoal jeans and an ivory silk shirt that made his dark good looks more foreign. 'Sit up and eat it while it's hot,' he added easily.

'I... You... Put it on the bed.'

'Joanne, don't be tiresome.' He sounded irritated and she really couldn't blame him; he must think she was more like a naive schoolgirl than a grown woman, she thought miserably. She dared bet his other women would be only too pleased to display their wares in similar circumstances, but then no doubt they wouldn't be caught looking like drowned rats in off-the-peg nighties. She just hadn't expected *him* to bring the food.

'There are two glasses; I thought we'd share a bottle of champagne while you eat to celebrate the beginning of the Christmas holiday,' he said coolly, watching her with narrowed blue eyes as she struggled up in the vast bed, the sheet wrapped round the top of her like a shroud. 'Are you cold?' he added mildly.

'No... Yes... I'm all right.' This was getting worse by the second.

'I'm not going to leap on you and have my wicked way.' It was said so conversationally it didn't register for a moment, but when it did she blushed scarlet. 'Relax, Joanne; you're making us both nervous.' There was a touch of steel in the coolness now.

It was all right for him, she thought testily. There he was, groomed to perfection as normal, calm, self-assured, perfectly in control, whereas she... The thought opened her mouth before she had time to consider her words. 'I...I look such a mess,' she said painfully. 'I didn't expect you to come.'

'Is that what's wrong?' he asked, the surprise in his voice telling her he hadn't considered such a possibility. 'Joanne, Joanne, Joanne...' He sat down on the bed, placing the tray at his feet before reaching forward and cupping her face in the palms of his hands. 'Don't you realise how beautiful you are, even freshly scrubbed and looking about sixteen?' he asked softly, the tenor of his voice making her shiver.

Freshly scrubbed and looking about sixteen! She gazed at him in frustration. She didn't *want* to look freshly scrubbed, she wanted to look alluring, voluptuous, sexy—like the other women he was used to. She wanted to dazzle him with her wit and sophistication, drive him mad with desire. She wanted—she wanted the impossible.

He bent down and picked up the tray, placing it on her knees before taking the cover from the plate to reveal a light meal of fluffy ham omelette and salad and baby new potatoes.

She stared at it miserably. She shouldn't have come. *She shouldn't have come.*

'Here.' He placed a wine glass in her hand before opening the bottle of champagne he had taken off the tray, its joyous explosion totally at odds with how she was feeling inside. 'Eat, drink and be merry,' he said mockingly, looking intently at her woebegone face. 'You're only stuck with me for a few days, Joanne; it isn't the end of the world.'

'I…I'm very pleased to be here.'

'You look it.' His voice was dark, grim even, as he poured her a glass of the sparkling effervescent liquid, before rising to his feet.

'Aren't you having one?' she asked quickly.

'Joanne, I know the image you have of me is of a womanising blackguard who hasn't got a sensitive bone in his body, but even I have my limits,' he said evenly, his face a study in controlled neutrality. 'We'll take this evening as a washout and try again tomorrow, okay?'

'Hawk—'

'And don't make any excuses; I really couldn't take them tonight.'

He was gone before she could say anything more.

CHAPTER NINE

'SO YOU'RE the Joanne Crawford I've been hearing so much about?'

It wasn't quite the opening line Joanne had imagined, and she found herself staring at Jed Mallen for a few moments before she collected herself and took the hand he was holding out for her to shake.

'Good afternoon, Mr Mallen,' she said politely, her heart beating a tattoo that was mercifully hidden from the bright blue eyes so like his grandson's, the direct, intent gaze seeming as though it wanted to get inside her head. 'I'm very pleased to meet you.'

'Likewise.' He had risen at her approach into the room, but now sat down again, saying almost irritably, 'Sit down, sit down, young woman; don't stand on ceremony.'

'Thank you.' She did as he bid but was unable to stop the colour from flooding into her cheeks. She hadn't known what to expect on meeting Hawk's grandfather—probably a bent old man who was showing the ravages of the illness he was battling against, if she had thought about it at all—but Jed Mallen was still tall and upright, virile almost, with a shock of springy white hair above a face that was handsome in spite of the lines of pain radiating from the piercingly clear blue eyes. She could see how this man had carved an empire for himself despite all the odds against him; Hawk was definitely a chip off the old block.

'Are you too warm?' Jed Mallen indicated the huge roaring log fire that was crackling in the fireplace of the beautiful, but very masculine, drawing room she had been shown into. 'The treatment I've been undergoing makes me susceptible to the cold, I'm afraid.'

'No, I'm not too warm, Mr Mallen; I'm afraid I'm one of those people who can never be too warm,' Joanne said quickly.

'Hmm, I can see why.' The laser-like eyes burnt up and down for a moment. 'You're too thin—or "slim", as it's supposed to be called these days. You don't live on lettuce leaves and carrots, do you?' he added caustically.

'No, I don't.' Joanne's hackles had risen and she answered smartly and with a marked lack of the ceremony he had spoken of earlier, her face stiffening tightly.

'And it's none of my damned business anyway.' He finished what she had left unsaid with a wry smile that was identical to Hawk's. 'Do you know, I think we'll get along just fine, Miss…? Can I call you Joanne?' he asked abruptly.

'Yes, of course,' she answered a little weakly.

'Thank you.' He sat back in the large winged leather armchair as he said, 'And my name is Jed, but of course you know that. Hawk isn't with you, is he?'

'No, there was an emergency in the San Francisco office this morning—'

'Yes, yes, I know; I arranged it,' he said briskly, with the touch of brusqueness she suspected was habitual with him, and then, as he caught sight of her look of surprise, added, 'You don't approve? He'll be back tonight, never fear—he is used to taking a plane here and there at a moment's notice—but I wanted to meet you for the first time without him around. Did you have a good flight?'

It was as though he had suddenly remembered his manners, and Joanne had to hide a smile as she replied, 'Very good, thank you.'

'Do you like my grandson, Joanne?'

'What?' She forgot this was the head of the Mallen

empire, a powerful, ruthless and, if half the stories about him were true, cruel multi-millionaire, and reared up in her seat as though she had been stung. What on earth had her liking Hawk to do with anything? she asked herself angrily. She was here as the manageress of Bergique & Son, wasn't she? And if he was doubting her ability to do the job—if he thought she had been sleeping with his grandson in order to get the position—

'I said, do you like my grandson?' The tone was flat, expressionless, and his face was perfect for playing poker. 'A simple yes or no will suffice.'

She stared into the hard, handsome face for a moment, the crackling of the fire, the subdued glow from the discreet lighting in the huge, sombre room, the absolute quiet beyond the walls all adding to the unreality of the moment. 'Yes, Mr Mallen, I like your grandson,' she answered quietly, in a tone as flat and even as he had used. 'He is a very fair employer.'

The formidably intelligent gaze roamed over her for a full minute—during which time she sat still and stiff with dignity—before he smiled, nodding to himself as he said, 'Yes, I understand now. You *are* different.'

'Different?' This extraordinary conversation was fast leaving the realms of reason. 'I'm sorry, Mr Mallen, but I don't understand—'

'Jed, my dear.' He adjusted his position in the chair, and she noticed the wince of pain he tried to hide with a rush of guilt and compassion. This was Hawk's grandfather and he was dying; she really shouldn't have got on her high horse—

'Would you take afternoon tea with me, Joanne?' He interrupted her racing thoughts quietly, not betraying by word or gesture that he had accurately read her thoughts. So she had compassion and tenderness, as well as guts, beauty and intelligence, did she? But of course she would have; he should have known...

'Thank you; that would be very nice.' Her earlier thoughts made her voice soft. 'Would you like me to show you some facts and figures I've brought with me?' She indicated the briefcase at her feet. 'And I've some financial statements—'

'Not necessary.' He waved the offer aside with the faintly irritable gesture she was beginning to recognise. 'Now I've met you I am quite happy to leave all that in your very capable hands.'

'But I thought—'

'Have tea with me, my dear.' He smiled, a real smile this time, which again was so like Hawk's rarely used but devastating smile that she found her breath catching in her throat. 'And we'll just chat, like two old friends, eh? I have little time for chatting these days, Joanne, and I am finding I want it more and more. You think that perverse?'

'No.' Now Joanne did smile. The old devil could use the Mallen charm when he cared to—he was even more like his grandson than she had first supposed.

'Ah, you think me manipulative.' The white head nodded at her. 'Don't bother to deny it; your face is very expressive. But you are right as it happens, although I am arrogant enough to view that particular facet of my character as an attribute rather than a shortcoming.' Now the smile was a grin, and Joanne actually laughed out loud at the somewhat wicked glee in the distinguished face.

She liked him. She hadn't expected to, not for a minute, but she liked this formidable, irascible old man very much, even as she understood how he had come to be so feared and held in awe by his contemporaries.

It was at the end of the afternoon she spent with Hawk's grandfather, after he had taken her on a slow tour of his fifteen-bedroomed mansion and they had had tea in the sumptuous and stylish drawing room, that he mentioned Hawk again.

'My grandson is wealthy and powerful and often pursued by predatory women; you are aware of this, Joanne?' he asked mildly, straight after a conversation spent discussing his fine antiques. 'Some of them have a mind of sorts, others are nothing more than empty-headed dolls, but they all have one thing in common— a desire to be seen with, and bedded by, Hawk Mallen. You are not like that. You are aware Hawk wants you?'

She had learnt enough during the afternoon about this amazing old man not to duck the question, but her cheeks were pink as she replied, 'Yes, I know he wants me.'

'But you don't want him?

He wasn't hostile, but Joanne still had to take a deep breath before she said, 'I...I don't think just wanting is necessarily enough, not without—without...'

'Yes?' He had moved forward in his chair, and now his voice was quiet and his eyes steady as he said, 'You can be honest with me, my dear, and you can also rest assured our conversation will go no further than these four walls. I will respect your confidence. What more is there beyond wanting?'

'Love,' Joanne murmured quietly, hot with embarrassment.

'Love. A small word but a big concept.' He leant back again, sighing deeply. 'I have loved two people in the whole of my life, Joanne; do you find that hard to believe?'

'No.'

She raised soft honey-brown eyes to his and he nodded slowly as he said, 'No, of course you don't; you have been hurt too.'

She waited, not knowing what to say, and after a minute had ticked by he said, 'I had an unhappy childhood, Joanne. I will not bother you with the details but suffice to say I did not love my parents. I met my wife when I was a nobody and she was a great lady, and we both knew instantly we were destined to be together. Her parents were horrified at the notion, obviously...' His voice was not bitter, merely matter-of-fact.

'She waited for me as I knew she would, and our marriage produced my son, Hawk's father, and took her life. I have often asked myself if my rage and bitterness at losing her so soon affected my relationship with my son, but I truly don't think so. I simply didn't like him. He was very like my own father in nature—cold, shallow, selfish—whereas Hawk's mother was a sweet girl, too sweet in retrospect. She allowed my son to get away with far too much.'

He paused, shifting his position in the chair again before he continued, 'I love my grandson, Joanne. I love him very much and I do not consider that emotion a weakness.'

'Hawk does.' She spoke before she could help herself, all her anguish and pain in the two words.

Jed looked at her for a few moments without speaking and then rose stiffly from the chair, standing with his back to her as he gazed into the leaping flames of the fire. 'I'm going to tell you a modern-day tale,' he said softly, 'a black fairy story if you like, and then it is up to you what you do with it.'

She said nothing, sensing that whatever he was about to do he wasn't doing lightly.

'Once upon a time a baby boy was born to a couple who appeared to have everything. There were no more children, so when the couple die in an accident, when the boy is a man, he has no siblings to stand with him in his grief. His sorrow at this time is not normal, because he has learnt things about his parents, dark, hidden things—things that have rocked his very foundations. Their death increases his already considerable wealth substantially, taking him into the super bracket and attracting women of the more...avaricious type. But he is not a fool, this man; he has lived with riches all his life and he knows their drawing power. However, one female comes along who is more clever than the rest, more...cunning. You follow me so far?' he asked quietly.

'Yes.' Her heart was thudding so hard it was echoing in her throat.

'He falls for her—lock, stock and barrel, as you English say. He needs someone at this time, someone who is wholly his, someone to take away the pain and uncertainty that came with the shock of his parents' untimely death and the subsequent revelations that were even more of a shock. And she knows this—oh, yes, she knows it all right—and she plays him like a virtuoso in the art of love—which indeed she is.'

She couldn't bear to hear it and yet she needed to hear it all; it explained so much.

'He asks her to marry him and she accepts—prettily, of course—and the invitations are sent, the presents begin arriving. And then he visits his best man one afternoon with some details about the wedding arrangements—he has known this friend since boyhood and he is more like a brother—and what does he find but his fiancée and friend flagrante delicto, in fact in the very act of copulation.'

Jed turned to face her then, the sapphire-blue eyes that he had passed on to his grandson blazing with rage in spite of it all being so long ago.

'The ultimate triangle—perhaps even funny if it wasn't so tragic. But worse is to come. Once word gets around about the broken engagement—and word gets around very fast in the sort of high-society circles this man moves in—several of his close friends are brave enough to tell him what they feared to say before—that it is not the first time this lady has been embroiled in a scandal. She has been involved with married men, had many lovers, both before and since knowing this man. It is not something a proud young man of twenty years of age wants to hear.'

'And...and this man—what does he do?' Joanne asked numbly.

'I think you know,' Jed said quietly. 'He becomes disillusioned, cynical, he takes the world by the throat and plays the game by his own rules, and in the process hardens and becomes cold, very much...very much like his grandfather,' he finished softly. 'But there is still the need to love and be loved there, hidden deep in the secret recesses of his heart, buried where no one can see it.'

'You believe that?' Joanne asked with painful directness.

'Don't you?'

'I...I think Hawk wants me because I am unattainable.' Joanne shifted restlessly in her seat. 'You have said yourself he is chased by some of the most beautiful women in the world—successful, rich women, women who are used to his lifestyle and enjoy it. Perhaps he just wants the thrill of the chase for once, to pursue rather than be pursued?'

'The man I was telling you about, the man in the story, is not a fool,' Jed said slowly. 'Perhaps when the one perfect jewel comes along he will recognise it for what it is.'

Joanne stared hard at the handsome face in front of her. Was he really saying he thought she was the right partner for his grandson, or was this incredible conversation a subtle suggestion to the contrary? If she was this 'jewel', Hawk certainly hadn't acknowledged it in the months she had known him and Jed Mallen must know that. Oh, she didn't know what to think, how to feel. She had enough problems struggling to keep her head above water with one cold, hard, enigmatic man, without taking on his grandfather too!

'I have enjoyed this afternoon immensely, but I must be going.' She stood up as she spoke and was going to hold out her hand for a formal farewell, but something in Jed's face—a fleeting sadness, a loneliness too deep and real for words—prompted her to lean forward on tiptoe and kiss his cheek. 'Thank you for sharing the...the story with me,' she said softly.

'Think about it,' he countered quietly. 'Please?'

'Yes, I will.'

She thought about nothing else as Jed's chauffeur drove her back to Hawk's home, but was left with nothing more concrete than a string of impossible questions.

Could anyone break through the ice that encased Hawk's heart? And if they did, would he want them for a lifetime, or just for a short while, until he became bored and restless? Could any female handle Hawk now that he had become so cynical and cold? She didn't feel she could, even if he wanted her for more than a brief fling. She didn't have a stable background to draw from, a well of family, or even worldly, knowledge. She wasn't clever or cosmopolitan or wealthy; she was just...herself. And it wouldn't be enough, *wasn't* enough.

By the time the long, luxurious limousine glided to a halt in front of Hawk's mansion she had faced reality. Dreams were one thing, real life quite another. She was torturing herself to no avail. She was just a passing whim to Hawk, a momentary obsession as he would term it, someone to have fun with as long as the mutual attraction lasted. And she couldn't be like that. She loved him far, far too much.

The next few days were a subtle combination of wild, fervent moments of happiness, grinding pain, poignant self-analysis and intensely fierce grief for what might have been. Hawk set out to make every minute of her Christmas memorable, and the fact that he succeeded only too well merely added to her turmoil until she began to wonder if she was becoming schizophrenic, especially as Hawk, after that first night, had become the perfect host—charming, attentive, courteous, amusing, and all the time remaining at a very controlled distance.

He had thrown a party for her on Christmas Eve which had begun with carol singers dressed in Victorian clothes and holding lanterns, and had finished, as the clock had chimed midnight, with warm glasses of mulled wine and hot mince pies.

On Christmas morning she had woken to a little Santa sack of presents at the end of her bed—she had no idea what time of the night he had placed it there—and he had come to sit on her bed with her and open the gifts, all the time being warm and friendly...and constrained. He had kissed her and wished her a happy Christmas, but it had been the kiss of a brother and made her want to scream.

They had spent the day with Jed, and Joanne had worn the ruby pendant and matching bracelet Hawk had given her—which must have cost a small fortune—and all the time she had been waiting for one sign, one word, to show she was something more than just— Just *what*? she had asked herself that night in bed. What was she? She wasn't a girlfriend, she wasn't a lover, she wasn't even a straightforward house guest. Jed had asked to see her and she had been brought for the audience with his grandfather post-haste. She'd cried herself to sleep.

It was on the afternoon of her last day in America,

when Hawk was driving her home after a day spent with some old—and, Joanne had discovered to her surprise, very normal and amusing—friends, and the sky was a river of purple and gold and scarlet, that things came to a head.

'Isn't it beautiful?' He had stopped the car on the top of a hill where the outlines of bare trees were silhouetted against the magnificent, colour-drenched sky, and it felt as if they were the only two people in the whole of the world. 'I often come here about this time of night when I'm home just to look at the sunset.'

'Do you?' She had seen this side of him more and more over the last few days—the softer, more vulnerable, gentle side of him. She had discovered he was a man who wasn't afraid to admit an appreciation of scenery and art, who could get on all fours and play with his friends' children like a five-year-old, who loved animals and was tender with anything weak and defenceless. She would rather not have discovered it—it didn't help her love to die—and die it had to.

'My mother used to come here too,' he continued quietly. 'She used to make the excuse she was exercising the dog, but after she died—' He stopped abruptly, taking a deep breath before he said, 'After she died, I understood why she needed to escape sometimes.'

'What happened to the dog?' It was an inane question, she realised immediately after she had said it, but the look on his face was breaking her heart.

'Bertie? He died shortly after my mother was killed.' Hawk turned from the windscreen to look at her then, his blue eyes silver in the twilight. 'He was an old dog; my mother had bought him when I started school—for company, I guess—and once she had gone he just sort of gave up. He adored her.'

'She must have been a lovely lady,' Joanne said softly.

'Yes, she was.' He flexed his long legs in the confines of the low, sleek sports car and turned fully to face her. 'Much like you.'

'Me?' Her breath caught in her throat before she reminded herself it didn't mean anything, not really.

'Yes, you,' he said huskily, his gaze sensuous. 'You—with your hair of fire and your big golden eyes; I want you more than I have ever wanted any other woman, Joanne—do you know that? And I have never trodden so warily, so carefully before.'

'You like the concept of the hunter after the prey?' she asked with painful directness.

'Prey?' The black brows beetled as he frowned. 'Is that how you see this? I don't think of you as a victim, Joanne, just the opposite in fact. I see you as a beautiful, desirable woman, but a woman who is more than able to hold her own in this crazy world we inhabit, and do it with integrity and courage too.'

Words, words, words, but what did they really mean? She stared at him, her face tense and unhappy. He was an enigma, this dark, cynical, cold man who had a drawing power so strong, so magnetic that it pole-axed lesser mortals, leaving them stunned and exposed.

'We would be good together, you know it, and I don't mean just the sex,' he said now, his handsome face shadowed and his hair blue-black. 'I want you with me, Joanne, *really* with me. I want to wake up in the morning and see you lying beside me, and know you'd be there in the evenings so we could discuss our days together. I want to eat with you, laugh with you, share the good times and the bad...'

'For...for how long?' she got out in a painful voice. This wasn't a proposal; she could see the darkness in those beautiful blue eyes that mirrored his soul.

'Does it matter how long?' he asked softly. 'Can't we take each day as it comes and be grateful for it, enjoy each other for as long as it lasts? I don't want to hurt you, Joanne. Trust me.'

'Hawk, I've told you before—'

'I'll look after you, Joanne,' he said evenly. 'You can be as independent as you want. I'll buy you a house, car, and set up an allowance for life that will make you financially secure and allow you to follow any path you choose.'

He didn't see. He really didn't see. She shut her eyes tightly for a moment, finding it was hurting too much to look at him. She didn't want to be independent or have an allowance or be wealthy for the rest of her life. She wanted *him*, she wanted a home they would share together, babies; she wanted—she wanted commitment, and she wanted it to be a willing commitment, because he loved her.

'Joanne?' She opened her eyes to see him watching her, his gaze tight on her face. 'You do care for me a little?'

She couldn't deny it but in the next moment, as his mouth swooped on hers, she realised she should have, because the second their lips touched sensation exploded between them like a raging fire, taking them both by surprise. His arms had closed round her fiercely, her own going round his neck as she pulled him even nearer, and as they strained together in the dim light from the setting sun the air inside the car was electric.

'You are mine; you know this; you cannot deny us both...' His lips were possessive as he murmured against the pure line of her throat before taking her mouth again in a kiss that was all fire and savage passion, and quite different from anything that had gone before.

She knew she had to resist the tide of thrilling sensation that was washing all reason and logic away, but it was hard, so hard, when she was becoming molten in his arms. He had just propositioned her—calmly laid out the ground rules and the benefits that would apply if she agreed to become his mistress. She *couldn't* give in now.

But in his own way he was being absolutely honourable. An insidious little voice was hammering away in her head, doing its part to break down her defences. Wouldn't it be better to take a relationship with him on his terms and hope that it might develop into something more—that one day he might find he couldn't do without her, that he loved her?

His tongue was doing incredible things to the soft contours of her mouth as his hands worked their own magic, and the feeling that was surging through her was so strong, so new and powerful, that she could barely breathe. She knew she was kissing him back with greater and greater passion, that all her body signs were leading him on to more intimacies, that she was stupid, *stupid*; but she couldn't stop.

He twisted in his seat, one hand moving between her shoulder-blades and the other into the small of her back as he drew her hard against the throbbing maleness of his body, her soft breasts crushed against the wall of his chest and her head thrown back to his searching mouth.

She could hear little moans—soft, inarticulate, sobbing groans—and it was with a tiny shock that she recognised they were spilling from her own lips, that her control was quite gone. And Hawk understood what was happening to her—it was there in the guttural growl deep in the base of his throat, in the way his hands moulded her slender frame to his as she clung pliant and shivering against him.

'You want me as much as I want you...admit it,' he murmured huskily against her flushed skin, his breathing harsh and ragged. 'You want me, Joanne; say it...

But it wasn't just wanting. She froze, the screaming warning her brain had been trying to give her for the last few minutes hitting home with savage force. She

wanted him because she *loved* him, and that meant she
wanted him a hundred times, a thousand times more than
he could ever want her. Her mother hadn't loved like
this—she couldn't have—because there was no way she
could have gone from man to man if she had. If she
couldn't have Hawk, *really* have him, in the only way
that would keep her sane—as lover, friend, companion,
husband—then she would have no one.

'Joanne?' Hawk's voice was questioning, the passion
that still had him in its grip making it throaty and harsh.

'I do want you, Hawk.' From some hitherto unknown
inner strength she forced herself to say what she had to
say. 'I want you very much, in a way I had never imagined wanting any man.'

'Joanne—'

'No, no, wait.' She interrupted his exultant voice
flatly, twisting back and away from him as she spoke. 'I
know now that you are the reason I've never wanted a
relationship with anyone else, that I was waiting—waiting but without knowing why.'

'And now you do?' he asked softly, the tenor of his
voice and the look on his face making it clear he knew
something was badly wrong.

For a moment, just one fleeting infinitesimal moment,
she contemplated preserving her dignity and pride—lying to him and making some excuse as to why she
couldn't become his mistress—but she couldn't. It had
to be all or nothing—she had known that from the day
she met him and fought against it for as long—and so
it was nothing because that was all Hawk could take.
Commitment, love, sacrifice—they were just words to
Hawk; he had torn the feeling that went with them out
of his soul fifteen years ago.

'Yes, I've known for some time,' she said quietly, her
eyes holding his and a wealth of pain at what she was
about to do making them as dark as night. 'I could never

become your mistress, Hawk, or your lover,' she continued quickly as he went to speak, 'because if I did it would destroy me, and probably you as well. You have your own moral code, I know that, and I don't think you would want to break someone deliberately.'

'Break you?' He drew back into his seat, his cold, handsome face straightening and his eyes taking on the piercing, diamond-hard sharpness that was so intimidating. 'What the hell are you talking about? I don't want to break you, Joanne. Damn it, you must know that.'

'I do.' She nodded slowly. 'That's the irony of it really.'

'Look, I've had enough of these riddles,' he said grimly. 'I want you and you want me, you've said it yourself, and we're two grown people, not a pair of giggling, groping teenagers,' he added bitingly. 'I've waited longer for you than I've ever waited for anything in my life, and I don't intend to wait a day longer.'

'You'd take me by force?' she asked tremulously.

'If I have to.' He glared at her, the swiftly darkening sky outside the window making him appear like a black silhouette with just the silver-blue of his eyes alive. 'But it wouldn't be by force a few seconds after I touched you, would it?' he continued relentlessly. 'We both know that. Damn it all, Joanne—' his voice had become a groan as his eyes took in the whiteness of her face '—what the hell do you want from me anyway?'

'The one thing you can't give or buy,' she answered tremulously, her love for him causing a physical pain in her chest that was excruciating. 'I don't care about a house or car; don't you see that, Hawk? And I don't want an allowance, or independence, or to follow my own selfish path. I want you, all of you—*I want it all*. I want to live with you, care for you, have your children, grow old together. I want to know you care for me as something more than a body or an attractive appendage on your arm for parties and dinners, that when I get my first grey hairs and my body begins to sag it won't make any difference.'

'Joanne—'

'No, listen,' she said fiercely. 'You listen to me. I don't want to have to wait for the phone to stop ringing, or worry about who you're with or what you're doing when you aren't with me. *I couldn't live like that*, don't you see? I want you to love me like I love you, and you can't, you can't,' she finished on a sob that almost choked her.

'You don't know what you're saying.' But his voice was shaky and he was perfectly still, the last glow from the dying sky outside the car windows strangely poignant to the moment.

'I know, Hawk.' She drew herself up proudly. 'I love you, hard as I know you'll find that to believe. And perhaps another woman could love you and still accept that the way you want it is the way it has to be, but I can't. I don't want you for a few months or a few years, I want you for ever, and to tell you anything different would be a lie. You've told me you always want the truth and that's the truth.'

'You're telling me you want a ring on your finger before you share my bed,' he stated flatly.

Joanne's face went still whiter but she forced herself not to flinch. 'No, that would be blackmail and quite useless with most men, let alone you,' she said shakily, willing the storm of emotion that was threatening to tear loose from the very core of her to be still. 'In fact if you asked me to marry you I would say no,' she continued bravely. 'A ring or a piece of paper means nothing if that's all it is, and it would be with you, I know that.'

'Then what the hell *do* you want?' he ground out savagely.

'I want you to let me walk out of your life,' she said

tautly. 'No recriminations, no bitterness, just a simple goodbye. And…and I want you to look around for another manager at Bergique & Son's. I'll…I'll stay till you've found someone else, of course, but then— Then I want to go.'

'You're telling me on the one hand that you supposedly love me, and on the other that you want to run out on me?' Hawk bit out with a fury that stunned her. 'What the hell sort of love is that?'

'My sort,' she said quietly, lifting her chin as she spoke.

'Then it stinks.' He grasped her shoulders, jerking her towards him. 'If you love someone, you're supposed to want to be with them,' he growled angrily.

'How would you know?' Suddenly there was hot molten rage flowing through her veins and she welcomed it, its cauterising power sealing her bleeding heart and allowing her to throw off his hands with an anger that matched his.

'I know.' He was breathing heavily, his eyes flashing blue fire. 'I was in love once, a lifetime ago, and I wanted to be with her but she had other ideas.'

'And so you let her go?' Joanne said quietly, her rage dying as quickly as it had been born. 'Well, that was love, wasn't it?'

'I let her go because I despised her.' His voice was as cold as ice. 'She betrayed me with a friend I loved like a brother; the two of them had been having an affair behind my back for weeks before I found out. But they lived to regret it; I made sure of that. And it taught me one thing, and for that I'm grateful—love is just another name for a physical act.'

'No.' Her voice was a whisper of pain. 'You loved someone who didn't exist, an image she'd projected. You never did love *her*.'

'What do you know about it?' he bit out cruelly.

'Your mother couldn't stop loving your father whatever he did,' Joanne said huskily. 'I'm sure she tried to—it would have made things so much easier, after all—but she couldn't, just as I couldn't stop loving you whatever you did. I don't want to love you, Hawk—in fact you are the last man in the world I would have chosen to love—but I can't help it. The only protection I have, the only thing I can do not to become like your mother—broken, tortured—is to live without you, to let go. That's what I meant when I said I wouldn't marry you even if you asked me; it would be history repeating itself, and I think you, even more than me, would find that abhorrent.'

'So it is over?' he asked with rigid control.

'It never even began.'

CHAPTER TEN

HER brave words—noble almost, she told herself with bitterly searing self-contempt—came back to mock her desperate misery once she was alone in her suite.

Hawk had driven home in the encroaching darkness without another word, his face as black as thunder and his hands gripping the leather-clad steering wheel so tightly, his knuckles had shone white.

He'd spoken briefly when they'd entered his home, and his voice had been curt and cold. 'I presume you would rather eat here than dine out?'

'Yes, please.' She had tried to match his detachment but failed miserably. 'Perhaps if I could have a tray in my room...?'

'What a good idea,' he'd said grimly. 'I will make sure Conchita is aware of it.' And then he had watched her as she had climbed the beautiful winding staircase, his eyes boring into the back of her head with every step she took.

If she had needed any confirmation that his heart was encased in stone, she'd had it this evening, she told herself miserably as she sat staring blankly into space in the magnificent suite of rooms. She had known he wouldn't exactly be overjoyed to hear that she loved him—still less that his plans to bed her had been thwarted—but surely one kind word, one understanding glance or even a sympathetic silence wasn't beyond him?

It was she who was suffering, after all—not Hawk. It was *her* heart that was broken, *her* feelings that were lacerated beyond repair... She gave herself up to a del-

uge of self-pity and despair. His pride had no doubt been
dented a little—his ego taking a bit of a hammering in
the process—but he didn't *love* her, so her refusal to
sleep with him was a momentary hiccup in his life, that
was all. And it wasn't as though she had refused him
because she didn't find him attractive or that she didn't
want him—she had told him how it was. The tears continued to flow, hot and acidic.

She was still struggling for composure when Conchita
knocked on her door half an hour later to enquire what
she would like for dinner, and she forced herself to listen
quietly as the little maid relayed several alternatives the
cook had listed.

'I don't mind, Conchita.' The thought of food was
repugnant anyway. 'Tell Cook I'll have whatever Mr
Mallen is having.'

'But Mr Mallen is having dinner at the Sandersons',''
Conchita said brightly, before stopping abruptly and
casting a glance at Joanne that clearly stated she was
worried she had made a gaffe.

'Oh, yes, I remember now.' Joanne found herself
speaking as easily and naturally as though she lied with
every other breath, and the fabrication must have been
convincing because Conchita relaxed again, bustling
away quite happily a few minutes later.

The Sandersons. She remembered the Sandersons: Mr
and Mrs Sanderson, filthy rich and full of their own im-
portance, and Victoria Sanderson—elegant, beautiful
and clearly crazy about Hawk. They had been at the
Christmas Eve party, and Victoria's black looks had left
Joanne in no doubt at all as to how the ravishing blonde
viewed Hawk's house guest.

So he had rushed off to seek solace with the voluptuous Victoria, had he? She found she was grinding her
teeth and it shocked her, bringing her shooting out of

her seat as though she were on springs. It didn't matter, it didn't; she wouldn't let it.

By the time Conchita brought the dinner tray at seven o'clock, Joanne had phoned the airport and made a reservation on a night flight to France; mercifully there had been a cancellation and a seat was available. It was the coward's way out—she knew that, she told herself miserably as she forced herself to swallow a few mouthfuls of the delicious dinner—but there was no way on this earth she could endure seeing Hawk tomorrow and travelling back to France with him as he had arranged. Besides, by relieving him of his duty towards her he could spend a few more days basking in Victoria's adoration if he wanted to, she thought painfully, bitter anguish making her as white as a sheet.

She was waiting in the hall when the taxi arrived, and slipped out quietly after leaving a note for Hawk thanking him for his hospitality, but saying in the circumstances she thought it better to leave at once. She also left the ruby pendant and bracelet.

She slept a little on the flight home, but the jangled nightmarish dreams were frightening and more exhausting than trying to stay awake, and by the time they landed, in the early hours of a cold and rainy Paris morning, she felt ill with a mixture of reaction and jet lag.

Once back in her apartment she fell into bed without bothering to undress, but in spite of falling into a deep, dreamless sleep as soon as her head touched the pillow she was awake again within a couple of hours, her brain dissecting every word that had passed between her and Hawk until she thought she would go mad.

She had showered, dressed, and left the apartment before eight, driven by a nervous tension so acute that she walked most of the distance to Bergique & Son, only riding the métro for the last part of the journey.

For the first time since she had been living there Paris

looked dull and dismal, the Parisians colourless and drab; in fact the very air seemed heavy and lifeless and defunct. It frightened her if she thought about it—this inert, joyless stupor that seemed to have taken her over since the conversation in Hawk's car—and so she was almost glad when, arriving at the office a day early, much to Antoinette's consternation, she found Pierre in her office rifling through the filing cabinet which had been locked when she'd left, and pure fury replaced the deadness.

'What are you doing?' It wasn't a time for social niceties and they both knew it.

The heavy-set Frenchman had swung round at her entry into the room, dropping the file he had been holding so the papers flew in a whirling arc about their feet, but he recovered himself almost instantly, the ingratiating smile she had seen once or twice before stitching itself in place. 'Joanne, we weren't expecting you—'

'*Je suis désolée, Pierre—*'

'Never mind saying you are sorry to him!' Joanne swung round so violently as Antoinette spoke behind her that the French girl actually backed away a step. 'It should be me you are apologising to, Antoinette. What on earth are you thinking of to let someone have access to my filing cabinet anyway?' she asked furiously.

'I can explain, Joanne.' Pierre's smile hadn't wavered. 'This is just a mistake.'

'I agree, Pierre, and I think you are the one who made it,' Joanne said cuttingly. 'You have no right to be in this building and you know it; I saw the contract Hawk made you sign and it is crystal-clear about that very thing. What is this file anyway?' She bent and picked up some of the papers from the floor, and in so doing missed the nod Pierre gave to his ex-secretary to close the office door so the three of them couldn't be overheard.

Joanne recognised the papers instantly; she had been working on the Netta Productions file prior to the Christmas break, and had begun to be very concerned about the matter before Hawk had whisked her away so abruptly. There had been the smell of something very nasty about the case but the facts had been buried in masses of red tape, and it had required patient and tactful digging to unearth the truth. Looking at Pierre's face as she raised her head, Joanne suddenly had the feeling she was staring at all the answers.

'Well?' Joanne stood up slowly, and it was only then that something very cold and very dark trickled down her backbone as she saw the look in the Frenchman's eyes.

'You stupid, arrogant Englishwoman.' He spat the words out of his mouth, following them with a string of profanities that were all the more menacing for being spoken so softly. 'You poke and you pry, do you not? You cannot leave anything alone.'

'*You* were responsible for that firm going bankrupt, weren't you?' Joanne said slowly, her intuition putting the last piece in the jigsaw. 'It wasn't their managing director who orchestrated the fraud, it was you, and you let an innocent man kill himself when the finger was pointed at him.'

'He was a weak fool.' Pierre's voice held not the slightest compassion. 'Now give me the papers, Joanne, and if you know what is good for you you will forget this conversation ever took place. I have many friends— friends who are invisible and can come and go at will; it would not be wise to cross me.'

'You're threatening me?' She couldn't believe it, she thought wildly. This was the sort of dialogue that belonged to an old second-rate movie, not an up-market publishing company at nine-thirty in the morning of a working day.

'But of course, this is one of the things I do so well.' Pierre flicked his head at Antoinette, indicating for her to leave the room, which she did with an alacrity that told Joanne the French girl was as scared as she was.

'You have only to say nothing and this whole unfortunate matter will die a death,' Pierre continued softly, walking across the room to stand in front of her, his dark eyes gleaming as he looked down into her pale face. 'That is not so hard, is it?' He put out a hand and raised her chin a little.

'Don't threaten me, Pierre.' His touch banished the fear that had had her in its grip, and put steel in her backbone. 'I won't be intimidated by you or anyone else. And don't touch me either.'

'No?' He considered her angry face with a slight smile. 'Perhaps I have underrated the little English girl, eh? Then what would you say to a more…agreeable solution? Perhaps a little thank-you in anticipation? Shall we say a figure of…?'

He mentioned a sum of money that brought her eyes wide open and her mouth slack, before she found her tongue. 'You think everyone is for sale, don't you, Pierre?' she said with icy and scathing disdain. 'Well, this may come as something of a surprise but I am not. These papers will go to the authorities, along with a report of our conversation today, and I think you might be viewing most of the new year from the inside of a prison cell.'

'I can't let you do that, Joanne.' His hands shot out to grasp her upper arms in an iron-like grip that was meant to terrorise. 'Don't make me hurt you—'

Take your filthy hands off her.

Pierre just had time to raise his head before he was plucked bodily into the air, and flung across the room with enough force to send him crashing against the far wall, where he landed with all the finesse of a stunned elephant.

'Get up.' Hawk's face was frightening. 'I'm going to teach you a lesson you'll never forget.'

'No, Hawk, no.' Joanne found she was actually hanging on to his back, her arms tight round his neck, as he tried to haul Pierre up by his jacket. 'Leave him, please; he's not worth it—'

'I'll kill the little rat.'

By the time help arrived a few moments later, summoned by Antoinette who appeared to have gone quite hysterical, it was clear Pierre was very glad to be led away and that threats and intimidation were the last thing on the Frenchman's mind, despite the fact that Hawk had told the two burly security men to hold him until the police arrived. Indeed he almost scampered out of the office, pulling the other men with him.

'You frightened him.' Joanne found she had to sit down very suddenly as the room began to swim and dip.

'I'd have done more than that if I hadn't had you round my neck like a limpet.' His voice was soft, very soft, and possessed a deepness that made her raise her head and try to focus on his face, a second before she found herself lifted up and cradled against his chest.

'Hawk, what are you doing...?'

'What I should have done a long, long time ago.' He marched across the room and into the outer office, past a weeping Antoinette and open-mouthed office staff, not saying a word until they were in the lift and going swiftly downwards.

'Hawk, I can stand—'

'Be quiet.' His voice was almost savage and he was crushing her against his body as though he was frightened to let her go, his heart pounding against the wall of his chest with such force it was shaking her frame.

Once in Reception they passed the two security men

and the chastened and silent Pierre without stopping, Hawk shouting a reply over his shoulder as they asked him where he was going.

'But Monsieur Mallen, the police—they will need a statement—'

'Damn the police.'

Hawk carried her over to his car once they were outside the building, depositing her in the front seat as though she were a piece of rare Meissen porcelain, and joining her inside moments later.

'Hawk—'

'In a moment, Joanne.' She subsided helplessly. He drove fast and furiously to a quiet spot overlooking green parkland, before bringing the car to a screeching halt and causing a flock of pigeons to rise in squawking protest. He cut the engine in the same moment and then turned and took her into his arms, ignoring her struggles as he swooped on her mouth in a kiss that seemed to draw her very soul.

'No, no, Hawk...' When she came back into the land of the living from the world of colour and light he had taken her into, she forced herself to try and escape his arms.

'Yes, yes, Joanne.' His tone wasn't mocking; in fact it was painful in its sincerity, his hands moving to cup her face as he stared down at her with the piercing blue gaze that was mesmerising. 'Please, darling, don't fight me.'

Darling? She stared at him, her honey-brown eyes huge. She couldn't be hearing right. 'I...I can't do this, I've told you.'

'Joanne, I love you; I've loved you from the moment I set eyes on you, and I shall die loving you,' he said huskily. 'I don't deserve you, I can never expect you to forgive me for the mess I've made of everything, but believe me when I say I love you.'

'You don't...you can't,' she murmured unsteadily, her ears buzzing as her senses swam again.

'I do, I can.' She hadn't realised she was crying until he caught a teardrop with his fingertip, his hands brushing her cheeks with a tenderness that took her breath away. 'I'm a stubborn man, my love, arrogant, foolish, but when I came home last night to ask you to marry me and you'd gone I got the next plane here.'

'You went to dinner with Victoria Sanderson,' she said shakily, unable to believe what was happening was real.

'No. I refused that invitation days ago, knowing it would be your last night in my home, but I forgot to tell Conchita and when I left so abruptly she just assumed I had gone there,' he said quietly. 'I drove for hours, trying to come to terms with all you had said and my own...my own personal demons. I realised I had been fooling myself, that I had been lying to myself for weeks—months—since the day we met. I didn't want an affair with you, Joanne, I wanted more, much more, than that, but I couldn't bring myself to accept it was love. It made me too vulnerable, too exposed, too much like the next man.'

'If...if that's true, then what made you change your mind?' she asked tremulously, not daring to believe it.

'You.' One word but his heart was in it.

'Oh, Hawk.' As her arms went round his neck their lips fused together in an embrace that brought flames of desire coursing hot and fierce, the world outside the car disappearing as reality became touch and taste and sensation.

'You forgive me, Joanne?' he groaned against the softness of her skin. 'I have no right to ask—'

'Yes, yes, I forgive you.'

'And you'll marry me? As soon as it can be arranged?' he murmured with desperate, hungry lips on her face, her throat. 'I want to care for you, my sweet love, cherish you, protect you. When I saw that gorilla holding you I wanted to tear him limb from limb.'

'I think he got the message.' Joanne smiled shakily through her tears, and then said, 'Hawk, are you sure?' She reached up and took his dark face in her small hands. 'Really, really sure?'

'I have never been so sure about anything in my life,' he said brokenly. 'You are everything I have ever dreamed of, everything I have ever desired. All that rubbish I spoke about love—damn it, Joanne, I was fighting myself, tearing myself apart inside. When you spoke about your childhood, the things you went through, it was like a knife tearing at my guts; I couldn't bear it. And still I continued to fight—'

'Hush.' She kissed the searing self-contempt and pain from his face, covering his skin in soft, burning little kisses. 'I don't care about the past; it's the future that matters.'

'And I promise you it will be a glorious one,' he said softly, his hands stroking her hair as his eyes devoured her face. 'A lifetime will be too short to tell you how much I love you. I didn't love my fiancée, Joanne; you were right about that and I knew the moment you spoke it out loud. It wasn't real love. Perhaps a desperation to belong to someone again, a need for reassurance after all that had happened with my parents, perhaps even the cry of a child in the dark—it was all those things, but not the lasting love of two people who are committed to sharing their lives together. It was never that. I have never loved any other woman before; I know that now. You have my word,' he finished seriously.

'And you never lie,' she said teasingly, her smile tremulous but full of joy.

'Only to myself,' he said soberly, clasping her close again, his arms so tight she could scarcely breathe.

'When you told me how you felt in the car, your beautiful face so white and haunted and your shoulders bowed beneath a burden that never should have been, the disgust I felt for myself was too much to bear. After all the torture of your early years, the pain you endured day after day in a loveless environment, you still had the strength to forgive and go on. It made me feel…contemptible, worthless. You had far more reason than me to shun love, to be afraid to reach out again, but you had done so—bravely and with such courage. Whereas I…'

'Don't punish yourself any more,' Joanne said shakily, distressed to see the pain and anguish in his eyes. 'We've both learnt from life, things we can pass on to our children and their children—'

'But first a time where I have you all to myself,' he said fiercely. 'I am a jealous man, my love; I cannot share you yet. I love you; I need to make you feel that, and I shall tell you every day of your life and beyond. You are mine as I am yours; I will always be everything you need. And our children will be brought up in the light of that love where the smallest shadow will not be allowed.'

Later, much later, when they had loved and touched and tasted and talked and the morning was gone, she moved drowsily in his arms as they continued to gaze out across the park, neither of them wanting to move back into the real world. 'What happened to your theory of women being good for one thing only?' she asked him mischievously, stroking the tanned skin of his chin where a dark stubble was already beginning to show.

'Did I say that?' The sapphire-blue eyes narrowed on her flushed, happy face. 'Well, in your case it is true— to love, worship and adore.'

'That's three things,' she protested weakly, the dark,

sensual glitter in the devastating gaze making her shiver with anticipation.

'I'll just settle for love, then,' he said softly, his hands beginning to coax passionate warmth into every nerve and sinew. 'True love is the greatest thing of all.'

HARLEQUIN ⬧ PRESENTS®

Passion™

Looking for stories that **sizzle?**

Wanting a read that has
a little extra **spice?**

Harlequin Presents® is thrilled to bring
you romances that turn up the **heat!**

In November 1999 there's **The Revenge Affair
by Susan Napier,** Harlequin Presents® #2062

Every other month there'll be a
PRESENTS PASSION book by one of your
favorite authors.

And in January 2000 look out for
One Night with his Wife by Lynne Graham,
Harlequin Presents® #2073

*Pick up a **PRESENTS PASSION**—
where **seduction** is guaranteed!*

Available wherever Harlequin books are sold.

HARLEQUIN®
Makes any time special ™

If you enjoyed what you just read,
then we've got an offer you can't resist!

Take 2 bestselling love stories FREE!

Plus get a FREE surprise gift!

Clip this page and mail it to Harlequin Reader Service®

IN U.S.A.
3010 Walden Ave.
P.O. Box 1867
Buffalo, N.Y. 14240-1867

IN CANADA
P.O. Box 609
Fort Erie, Ontario
L2A 5X3

YES! Please send me 2 free Harlequin Presents® novels and my free surprise gift. Then send me 6 brand-new novels every month, which I will receive months before they're available in stores. In the U.S.A., bill me at the bargain price of $3.12 plus 25¢ delivery per book and applicable sales tax, if any*. In Canada, bill me at the bargain price of $3.49 plus 25¢ delivery per book and applicable taxes**. That's the complete price and a savings of over 10% off the cover prices—what a great deal! I understand that accepting the 2 free books and gift places me under no obligation ever to buy any books. I can always return a shipment and cancel at any time. Even if I never buy another book from Harlequin, the 2 free books and gift are mine to keep forever. So why not take us up on our invitation. You'll be glad you did!

106 HEN CNER
306 HEN CNES

Name _____ (PLEASE PRINT)

Address _____ Apt.# _____

City _____ State/Prov. _____ Zip/Postal Code _____

* Terms and prices subject to change without notice. Sales tax applicable in N.Y.
** Canadian residents will be charged applicable provincial taxes and GST.
  All orders subject to approval. Offer limited to one per household.
  ® are registered trademarks of Harlequin Enterprises Limited.

PRES99 ©1998 Harlequin Enterprises Limited

EXTRA! EXTRA!

The book all your favorite authors are raving about is finally here!

The 1999 Harlequin and Silhouette coupon book.

Each page is alive with savings that can't be beat!

Getting this incredible coupon book is as easy as 1, 2, 3.

1. During the months of November and December 1999 buy any 2 Harlequin or Silhouette books.

2. Send us your name, address and 2 proofs of purchase (cash receipt) to the address below.

3. Harlequin will send you a coupon book worth $10.00 off future purchases of Harlequin or Silhouette books in 2000.

Send us 3 cash register receipts as proofs of purchase and we will send you 2 coupon books worth a total saving of $20.00 (limit of 2 coupon books per customer).

Saving money has never been this easy.

Please allow 4-6 weeks for delivery. Offer expires December 31, 1999.

I accept your offer! Please send me (a) coupon booklet(s):

Name: _____

Address: _____ City: _____

State/Prov.: _____ Zip/Postal Code: _____

Send your name and address, along with your cash register receipts as proofs of purchase, to:
In the U.S.: Harlequin Books, P.O. Box 9057, Buffalo, N.Y. 14269
In Canada: Harlequin Books, P.O. Box 622, Fort Erie, Ontario L2A 5X3

Order your books and accept this coupon offer through our web site
http://www.romance.net
Valid in U.S. and Canada only.   PHQ4994R

HARLEQUIN PRESENTS®

*invites you to see
how the other half marry in:*

SOCIETY WEDDINGS

This sensational new five-book miniseries invites you to be our VIP guest at some of the most talked-about weddings of the decade—spectacular events where the cream of society gather to celebrate the marriages of dazzling brides and grooms in breathtaking, international locations.

Be there to toast each of the happy couples:

Aug. 1999—**The Wedding-Night Affair**, #2044, Miranda Lee

Sept. 1999—**The Impatient Groom**, #2054, Sara Wood

Oct. 1999—**The Mistress Bride**, #2056, Michelle Reid

Nov. 1999—**The Society Groom**, #2066, Mary Lyons

Dec. 1999—**A Convenient Bridegroom**, #2067, Helen Bianchin

Available wherever Harlequin books are sold.

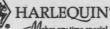

HARLEQUIN®
Makes any time special™